E

The Seeker's Burden

AN EMERGING THREAT

Mark E. Lein

Published by BorderLein Publishing.

Cover Illustration by Glen Wilkinson

Special thanks to Megan Riddle for editorial support and the creation of the map, to Doug Riddle for editorial support and excellent typesetting. Also thanks go out to John Lein and my wife Emily for the editorial support and guidance throughout the process.

ISBN-13: 978-1493592890 · ISBN-10:1493592890

Dedicated to Emily, Oliver, Lucy.
My heart is yours.

The Tri-Islands

CONTENTS

1
IT BEGINS

OLIVER BREATHED IN THE mist clinging to the black rock of the Citadel ramparts and drank in the comforting silence. He raised his hand and blue fire arced from his gloved fingers to illuminate the walkway as he moved slowly across the northern wall. Astar nobles had arrived on the Island and he wanted to be as far away from the High Chamber as possible. The recent increase in interaction between the Seekers and the militant Astar was beginning to concern him. His people were one of solitude and learning, reaching out to the rest of the world only when something critical to the completion of research was needed. He had begun to feel an underlying tightness in the Citadel's community, more so when he spoke to his father or other members of the Council.

As he passed through the archway of the North-west tower he heard a slight scrambling sound coming from the base of the outer walls. When he leaned over the edge to look for the source, his world turned a brilliant and soundless white. Stumbling back, he fought to stream power into a protective web.

As his eyesight returned he found himself curled against the rampart wall with the shimmering shield he had raised still intact around him. He stood and tried to catch his breath as he allowed the protective energy to dissipate. Pain shot through his head as his hearing began to return in a high pitched whine. The pitch suddenly changed and became louder, but then he realized it wasn't coming from his head at all. He began to hear the screams that echoed from inside the Citadel walls.

Trying to make sense of the maddening sounds erupting from below, Oliver raced along the rampart. Coming to the stairway that led down into the courtyard of the Citadel, he found it obscured with dense smoke. Tongues of fire began to fill his vision, quickly spreading through the lower dwelling areas. In panic he leapt down, leaving the clear moonlight and entering dark madness. Huge black shapes moved in the smoke as screams and the pealing sounds of metal striking metal and stone echoed mutely off the walls. Turning towards a nearby wall for cover, Oliver slipped in a slick of dark liquid and crashed onto a limp form lying at the entrance of one of the surrounding houses. He barely had time to glimpse the body's ravaged face–and recognize a council member, before something massive grabbed him by a leg. Oliver was thrown across the cobblestones and came to a jarring landing skull first against a marble column. Smoke, fire, and cries of pain and anger faded into blackness.

O LIVER WAS A SEEKER-IN-TRAINING, born into a human community that nearly worshiped science. Academics by trade, the Seekers were the land's most famous and highly regarded scholars, focusing on the study of solar energy and its uses. Reclusive to a fault, they rarely left the Black Island.

Born to an Academic council member, Oliver grew up in the confines of the Sun Fire Citadel on the Black Island, knowing little of the world without. His father told him many stories of travels and adventures of generations past, but did not encourage the same for his son. By the time he was eight years of age Oliver had attempted to run away innumerable times. Every time he was found out, sometimes fished from the water of the lake that surrounded the small island, he would plead and argue that he was meant to see what lay beyond the Island. Finally at a loss, his father entered him into the Solar Circle, the school of the Seekers, using his position to bend the rules of age required for admission. Oliver was welcomed by the leading scholars due the status of his family, but his fellow students were often jealous and left him in seclusion much of his years of study.

Despite this, he excelled, picking up the scientific algorithms and the understandings of the solar domain at a bewildering pace. Noting his prodigy, the Circle made him the apprentice of Magnus, who in younger years had been seen as the greatest of the Order. Under his tutelage, Oliver grew into a young man with an understanding and thirst for learning that strained at the limits of Magnus himself.

This understanding of the solar realm, and the responsibilities that were laid on him by his tutor, began to feed into Oliver's childhood fantasies of leaving the Island. The vastness of the sky world only made his feel cramped. He felt constrained in a perpetual training environment and dreamed of using what he knew to help others. The situation of late did nothing to curb his desire, as details of inter-tribal warring on the High Plateau and mysterious disappearances in the Northern Lowlands filled reports that flowed into the citadel. A near famine had been spreading through the Astar lands as well.

During the last few months, there had been a steady stream of high ranking Astar dignitaries to and from the Island, and meetings with the Citadel's leaders lasted through the night. At first, intrigued enough to attempt spying on the events, Oliver had been unable to break past the defenses. As time passed and the meetings became more common he lost interest.

O LIVER WOKE WITH THE morning sun struggling to wind its way through the dense haze of smoke and ash. Curling up as pain radiated through him, he fought to remember what had happened. Touching his head he felt hair matted with dried blood. He slowly forced himself to stand and found himself surrounded by the bodies of council men and Astar noblemen in royal blue, bodies torn apart and tossed like driftwood with blood splattered on the cobblestones. Once bright armor was rent and broken; blades shattered and thrown about. The stench of death and gore threatened to unhinge his insides and he used his cloak to cover his face.

In the midst of deafening silence Oliver forced himself to ignore bloodless and familiar faces as he slowly made his way across the courtyard towards the wide doors of the Citadel's high council chamber. The great timbers were splintered and hanging from battered iron cross bars. As he stepped through the gore strewn courtyard Oliver searched the ground for a weapon of some kind in case the attackers were still about. The sun flashed off metal, leading him to a short sword with jeweled hilt lying next to the body in the uniform of an Astar General. He took the sword and raised it awkwardly, the weight forcing him to use both hands. So armed, he continued to the council doors and listened for any sound coming from within. Profound silence welcomed his ears and he made his way into the cavernous entrance hall using what meager light came through the doorway.

A cry of pain suddenly echoed from the darkness ahead making him drop the sword in panic. The clatter of the steel choked off his breath. For many moments he crouched against a side wall, fighting to quiet his heartbeat. A second, quieter cry made him jump to his feet in recognition and he stumbled through the darkness until he could no longer see the guiding walls. He held out his gloved hand and pressed a hidden thumb stud, holding it down as a stream of blue fire silently boiled into an orb that he tossed to hover near the ceiling of the central meeting room of the Citadel.

Oliver's breath caught in his throat as the cool light illuminated an even greater scene of slaughter than that in the courtyard. Nearly every surface was drenched in blood or blackened with fire and the bodies of his kinsmen and Astar alike were strewn everywhere. The carnage was concentrated around a massive black hulk lying in the center of the room. As he crept closer he made out the muscled limbs and thick armored body of a creature that must have stood over twice the height of the largest of men. The face was long and reptilian, the dead eyes yellowed and catlike, its jagged jaw lined with razor teeth. Its long limbs ended in great blood stained claws and the entire body was scaled. Hafts of broken spears, sword blades, and countless arrows were sticking out of its body, evidence of the massive effort taken to bring it down. The pure malevolence emanating from the body even in death made him keep his distance.

Remembering the cry, Oliver searched the surrounding bodies for the face of his tutor. Seeing movement he ran to the side of yet another bloodied body. Magnus lay as though every bone in his body were crushed, molded to the broken stone beneath. Blood soaked his long robes and when Oliver placed his hand gently to his chest, there was but a shallow breath coming through cracked lips.

Oliver started as Magnus' eyes strained open and his mouth gaped with silent words, little more than a gurgle reaching his ears as he bent close to the dying man. "Use the key" came the whisper, the words spoken again and again until Oliver repeated it back. With great effort, Magnus dragged a ruined arm towards Oliver and within his open hand lay a large bronze key of ancient make. Seizing Oliver's gaze with his blazing and dying eyes Magnus gave one more breath to the words, "Use the key", and collapsed with a sigh as life faded away. Stunned, Oliver stood and walked unsteadily back out into the courtyard, key in hand. He stood at the doors, unable to think, his mind attempting to seal his sanity against the encroaching madness.

With a sudden cry he burst into a sprint towards the Citadel's housing areas, dodging burnt timber and vaulting bodies. The same devastation was everywhere, blood pooling and in some cases even forming small streams through the pathways. Skidding to a stop he stared in horror at what was left of the home he and his father shared. Shuddering with panic and dread, he made his way through the rubble until he saw the body.

2
SHATTERED REALITY

Oliver came to his senses hours later, kneeling in the wreckage of his home. Slowly rising to his feet, he stumbled back through the ashes and destruction to find other survivors. All he found was silence and the rancid stench of death.

He walked through the entire Citadel and down through the fields where the food was grown, ending at the docks. Every boat seemed to be disabled, some fully submerged with only masts showing in the dark water. Oliver began to lose himself, his mind turning against him. He needed someone to talk to, to verify his own existence. It began to feel like a dream. Yes, he thought, that is what this is. What this has to be. Yet he could not wake no matter what he tried, and his mind began to turn on itself. Whispers of madness echoed like thunder in his ears as he wandered back to the main courtyard, hands running along walls for support.

By the time he arrived, he had gained a bit of himself back. Reaching into the pockets of his cloak, he pulled out a sphere of iridescent stone and cupped it in both hands. Breathing on it softly caused the stone to radiate heat and pulse with bluish light. Holding it close to his chest Oliver let the reassuring heat wash through him, the healing light chasing the whispers away. After several seconds, knowing the importance of the stone and its limited energy, he grudgingly placed it back into one of his many pockets.

Somewhat refreshed, he looked once more upon the slaughter radiating out from where he stood, towards the council doors. Mind clearing, he began to notice things out of place. There were pools and smears of a dark viscous substance here and there throughout the ruined bodies, evidence that something inhuman had bled there. Then there was the nature of the wounds on the bodies; ragged gashes mingled with clean cuts made by bladed weapons.

It looked as if the attacking force had both creatures like the one lying inside the meeting hall and others that used more traditional weapons. There was evidence of a large group of people (or some other beings) moving among the carnage, seemingly to move bodies or equipment. Large bodies looked to have been dragged through pools of blood and the marks led towards the southern shore of the island.

Following the trail, Oliver made his way through the education centers and to the water's edge. Heavy, metal clad feet had bruised the ground and broken shale for a hundred yards to either side of where he stood. There were long poles, taller than he was, stuck into the shore at even intervals of ten paces. Remnants of rope and chain dangled from metal eyes in the tops. He inspected one more closely and discovered the poles were covered with curved hooks made to secure them in the ground. Oliver was confused as to how such things had been placed and for what purpose. On one, the chain stretched into the water and he strained to pull it towards him until the end came into view. It was welded to a section of wood and iron that looked to have been part of a vessel bulwark of some kind.

Thinking that this meant that the poles had been used to tie boats in place, Oliver completed his quick search of the surroundings. He began to wander, letting his feet take him where they would, until he remembered the key. Magnus had given him a key and had told him he must use it, but what lock would it fit?

Thinking as he walked, he made his way through the citadel towards the lodging terrace where Magnus had kept a small room. The door was in place but opened easily as he pushed against it. He had been inside many times throughout his apprenticeship and he now had an idea of what to look for. There had been a hiding place of some kind that he had come across when he was a boy. The result of his discovery had been a stern discussion and a triple workload that week. Though he had stayed away after that, he had never forgotten its location.

Moving to the small bed he lifted and pulled it away from the stone wall. At the base of the wall, where the stones met the wooden planks of the floor, was a recess not much larger than a keyhole. Taking the key from his cloak, he pushed it into the opening until it hit something solid and tried to turn it. At first nothing happened, but he pushed harder until he felt something shift and a hidden mechanism clicked.

A four foot section of the wall recessed slightly and, as Oliver pushed it, slid aside on some sort of oiled rail system until the opening was large enough for him to slip inside. In darkness, except for the light coming in through the windows behind him, he triggered his thumb stud and sent the stream of fire before him.

He nearly bumped his head on the low ceiling of the alcove when his flame jumped towards the floor and was swallowed by a glass-like sphere. In the near-darkness he watched as the glass began to glow brighter, using the fire's energy to illuminate the ground. It sparked as the light began to run from the glass along a thin copper cable to fill yet another sphere a few feet ahead.

It continued to spread until the cable turned a corner and left his view. He stood at the entrance for a minute, surprised at the breadth of the passage, wondering how it fit into the building and where it might lead. After glancing once more back into the room he began to follow the dim blue light.

Taking the corner he nearly fell down the steep steps that chased the light in a gentle curve as it fell from sight. He descended the steps for long minutes as they curved in a lazy spiral deep into the Island. He was breathing hard when he finally saw the lights level out and illuminate a wide corridor leading to a doorway. Stepping through the entrance he again was startled when the light, that had been following the ground, jumped up and away from the wall until it entered a much larger sphere high above.

Darkness enveloped Oliver and he was about to use his flame again when light erupted around him, streaking from one sphere to another until the cavern that lay before him was bright as day just turning to dusk. The ceiling stretched high above and the walls disappeared into the distance. A set of flagstone steps led from the doorway to a stone table that stood next to a small pool of dark water. Water dripped in languid drops from crevices high above, causing the pool waters to ripple in constant motion.

Crystal running through the cave walls gleamed in the hazy light. The only sound was the echo of the water droplets impacting the pool and the surrounding stone. Oliver slowly made his way down the wide steps and stopped at the table. Made entirely of hewn stone, the table was low and supported a long rectangular chest made of cedar and banded with iron. An ancient lock hung from the clasp.

It was like no lock he had ever seen. There was no hole, no indent or space to insert anything, let alone a key. It looked to be made of some kind of reddish crystal shot through with twists of silver and there was nothing to suggest how or where it was secured. It threaded its way through the clasp like a living thing and folded over into itself.

Looking around for ideas, Oliver spotted a lean-to across the cavern in a shadowed recess in the stone. Making his way past the pool he saw that it must have been lived in at some point. A moldy straw mattress and several wool blankets lay heaped underneath the moderate protection of the wooden planks that formed the shelter.

Nestled in the center of the heap of blankets was a lump of darkness. Reaching down Oliver picked up the object, or stone as it turned out. It was as smooth as glass and pitch black with no discernible edges so that it looked as if he had a hole through his palm. Peering closer he made out the faintest of glimmers, orange streaks swirling under the surface. As he brought it out into the light the orange brightened and moved faster. A steady heat began to emanate from the stone and he hurriedly placed it on the stone table next to the chest.

When he did, a curious thing happened. The crystal lock on the chest strained towards the black stone. That is the only way his mind could interpret it. It was like a living thing, changing its shape, elongating until it touched the stone. Sparks flew at the contact and Oliver jumped back as the crystal wrapped itself in a flow of metal and stone around the dark rock, separating from the chest.

The thing sat there, still now and as gray as any

ordinary gravel, the heat of its movement dissipating quickly. Oliver reached towards the chest.

3
DARK CREATURES

DAYS EARLIER, IN THE wastes of the High Plateau, Ethan's sword struck an upraised shield in a shower of sparks, sounding a peal of thunder that echoed off the surrounding trees. His adversary, a towering Savoq warrior, grunted in pain, shield falling from the arm shattered by the blow. Ethan spun out of reach of the wild retaliatory swing of the Savoq's short sword and allowed the weight of his greatsword to bear him back to slice through his enemy's now unprotected side, nearly halving the Savoq's body. Crouching, he let the dead warrior fall from his blade as he searched for his next opponent.

Surrounded by Savoq dead and wounded, Ethan silently waited for the remaining score of tribal warriors stalking towards him. A bright flash of color caused him to turn; searching through the mass of brown leather clad bodies till he caught sight of the glistening silver and royal blue of his only companion's armor and tunic.

Whispering the Prayer of the Warrior for his fallen comrade, Ethan resolutely stood to face the raiders' charge. As he braced for the impact, there were flashes of movement in the surrounding trees. The Savoq bringing up the rear of the attacking force were swept like leaves into the darkness of the wood by blurred shapes that whispered through the periphery of his vision. Then the surrounding forest exploded, branches snapping and popping, as a chorus of chilling predatory cries froze the fighting men in place.

ETHAN WAS A PRINCE of Astar. The eldest of four brothers and with no desire to hold a position of political power, he strained at the boundaries placed on him through his blood. Early in his life, a certain martial ability caught the attention of Blash, one of the Oskara Arch-Knights. This led to his entrance into the Oskara apprentice program at the age of seventeen. Though seen as a great honor by the Astar public, his family and other political leaders looked down upon his choice. The Queen had been the only one to side with him but she had died shortly after. His father, King Luitger, refused to talk to him and his greater family mocked his choices. They read his actions as a betrayal of their noble name as direct descendants of the original human race to first come to Astar from across the Beryl Sea, innumerable generations ago.

The Oskara he joined were handpicked warriors that filled the coveted position of high protectors of Astar. Unmatched in battle they are looked upon by the Astar people as the backbone of their military might. Lauded as heroes and lords, they are supplied with the best armor and weapons forged by the famed Goblin blacksmiths of the western hill country.

The brotherhood of the Oskara was formed around three tomes of aspiration; Control, Honor, and Mastery which are the framework for the rigorous training apprentices receive. Only the most experienced Oskara Knights who become skilled in specific tomes are named Weapon Masters, acting as the trainers of the elite force. In time of war, they also act as troop commanders for the Astar armies, lending their expertise to the more common soldiers.

Ethan allowed the pain of his family's ostracism to fuel his desire to excel in training. In a short time he was given command of a small squad of Oskara and became known throughout the countryside. In the years following his induction into the Oskara order, he also gained a rather skeptical reputation of dealing with renegade Seekers and attempting to gain their knowledge for use in battle.

A week before, Ethan was sent on a diplomatic mission to foster peace between the Savoq tribes and to establish trading agreements between them and his people. He was chosen by his father for this task, as despite the schism between them, the king never hesitated to use the skills his son possessed.

ETHAN WAS THE FIRST to move, throwing himself into the scrub brush just as the things stalked out of the trees. They were like nothing he had seen in this world, black as a night with no moon, they seemed to suck the light away. Standing upright and roughly man-shaped, the creatures were covered in scales and their forelimbs ended in pincer-like claws, eyes glowing a deep amber. They were short in stature with lean, muscular frames.

The lead creature opened its ragged mouth and a chattering laugh like steel dragged across gravel bubbled out. The Savoq warriors didn't have a chance to react before the creatures charged into their midst, claws ripping through throats and unprotected flesh.

From his hiding place, Ethan pressed himself

into the dirt and watched in horror as the band of Savoq was destroyed in mere seconds. The creatures weaved through the one-sided melee, quick as the absence of light.

As the last Savoq fell, the creatures darted back into the darkness of the surrounding trees, silence following. After waiting an interminable time to ensure the creatures had moved off, Ethan quickly moved to the body of his comrade, Kael. He dragged him the hundred yards to where they had hidden their horses at first sign of the Savoq raiding party. They had been attacked as they searched the trampled ground for clues to where the raiders were heading.

He wanted to put as much distance between himself and the black things. Grunting with the effort, he shoved the limp, armored form onto the large bay that nickered and sidestepped in response to the smell of blood. Once he had secured the body with rope, Ethan mounted his pitch black stallion named Whisper. Urging him to a fast trot, Ethan called out for the bay to follow. He headed north as the sun began to fall towards the plains.

His mission of establishing trade and working towards peace could wait. He had witnessed something so dark that he couldn't begin to understand it. Even now his mind played tricks with the memory of the black things, the forms twisting until he all he could be sure of was the pure evil that had emanated from them. An icy fear had seemed to reach out from the amber eyes, chilling his very blood.

He decided to go back to the capital, Astar Terrace, and seek the counsel of ones who had more wisdom. He knew he must also bring a warning of the new danger to his father. Hopefully he would find an audience possible under the circumstances.

4
SECRETS BELOW

THE CHEST DID NOT open easily. Rusted shut, it took all Oliver's effort to wrench it open. With a crack and a spray of dust the lid fell back, exposing the contents. Stacks of documents lay in ordered layers. A book with a battered leather cover nestled next to a long dagger with a crystal fitted to the pommel.

There were markings on the book that tugged at his memory, he had seen this book before. He had seen Magnus carry it many times, often writing in it. Oliver remembered that when he would ask about the book he would receive a grunt in response and it would disappear quickly in Magnus' robes. He gently took it out of the chest and untied the leather strap that held it closed.

The pages were filled with scribbled text and crude sketches of graphs and equations that he did not understand. He quickly flipped through it and noticed that all the pages were completely full, though in the last few pages the text was straighter and more concise. Setting it back on the table, he reached into the chest and took out the stacks of documents, arranging them across the stone.

Jagged shapes and portions of words filled the pages in a disordered mess. Stepping back from the table, Oliver tried to make something out of the jumble. Just when he was about to give up he remembered something. Years ago Magnus had given him puzzles to work out in his free time, stressing the usefulness of such an exercise. It gave him the ability to see disparate objects or ideas and combine them into something understandable.

Magnus had said to be able to do this was critical for people in places of leadership, allowing them to pare through the enormous amounts of information continually thrown at them, formulate coherent thoughts and provide direction to their subordinates. Grinning, Oliver reached down and began to rearrange the pages. Starting with one, he looked for another that had any corresponding markings. Eventually he found one that fit, completing several words and continuing some kind of faded image.

An hour, and a sore back later, he sighed and stood back from the stone table. Spread out before him, roughly six feet by four, was a map.

A notation at the bottom of the nearest page drew his gaze. The words were small, unlike the giant ones that covered the rest of the pages. He read the following:

As by light you may understand, so by darkness will the truth be revealed.

Scratching his day-old beard growth, he scanned the pages again for any sign of similar notations for further guidance, without success. As he thought he reached back into the chest and pulled out the dagger. The weight surprised him, dragging his hand toward the cave floor. Grunting with the effort he placed it on the documents and inspected the weapon.

It had a black translucent blade, silver cross hilt, and a wire wrapped handle, but it was the pommel that took his attention. Glowing amber with scarlet streaks, the stone seemed alive. Moving so that the light could better hit the dagger, he touched the gem with his gloved hand.

An explosion rocked the cavern, a reverberating crack as if the very fabric of being had been torn. Reeling back, Oliver closed his eyes against a glaring light and tried to maintain his footing as the ground seemed to shift beneath him. Silence. Sudden silence. Piercing silence. The instant removal of chaotic sound seemed to bring more pain than the sound itself. Head pounding, Oliver opened his eyes to near darkness. The lights above had gone out, leaving the glowing pommel as the only source of illumination.

Sudden movement pulled his gaze from the glowing dagger to the parchment laid out on the table. It was moving. Not as if by a breeze, there was none, but moving as if alive. One by one the pages rippled and whispered across the stone towards each other. As he bent closer the light from the dagger seemed to stimulate the pages, causing them to speed their movement. They shrank as they began to join together, edges merging as if like liquid metal. Breathless, he watched the living parchment become a single page. As the movement ceased, the light from the pommel stone leapt towards the ceiling and the cave lights were illuminated once more.

The words and images that covered the page came into focus, revealing what appeared to be a map. There were notations scrawled across it, as though the creation of it had taken many attempts. The text was in a tongue no longer used in the known world, though it was the first of the old languages that he had been taught by Magnus. That thought caused a chill to run down his spine as Oliver had the feeling that the map had been meant for him.

The map itself showed the basic shape of the Tri-Islands with a trail marked leading from the Citadel into the Shadowmyst Mountains. This largely unexplored range perched on a large island off the west coast of the mainland. The path was titled simply "truth". He began to read the text, beginning with the words lining the top of the page. In order of reading:

> *For the day of dire events, these words shall*
> *be for the one to come and unearth the power*
> *of truth. My labor long, I have toiled towards*
> *this day, only to glimpse it from the grave.*
> *Take on the mantle of pain and rid the world*
> *of falsehood.*

To the side of the marked trail the text began to read like a set of directions in a more concise hand.

> » *From island of firelight to towering hills, the*
> *sun will be at the back during the hour of*
> *dawn. A half turn to the right will keep you*
> *straight as you go.*

> » *Welcome will be met at the mouth of a cave and help will follow.*
> » *Across the Narrow Sea will the path go, to reach the land beyond.*
> » *West and higher, until the land is laid out before you, into the darkness of storied past.*
> » *Guidance will be forced upon, action to be decided.*

The remaining words struck a memory in Oliver's mind. He remembered hearing Magnus muttering it under his breath countless times.

> *When given the choice, flee. But flee into pain, not to safety that lies in wait to ensnare for eternity. To you is given the most powerful gift, opportunity to understand more so than any before. Look to the bearer of sadness but do not be hindered by whispers of fame. Fame is a tool of darkness. Be unknown and do what is required. The truth is ready to be revealed.*

There the text ended. Oliver re-read the parchment again and again until he memorized it, though he was far from understanding it. The one thing he did understand was that there was no reason to stay in the Citadel.

5

BORDER TROUBLE

JUST AS OLIVER CAME to that realization, Ethan rode over the draw-bridge and entered the soldier's quarter of Astar Terrace. As he guided Whisper and the following bay mare towards the nearby stables a voice boomed from the entry of the gate-house. Grinning, Ethan turned to see his friend and mentor.

An older man, Blash was one of only a small handful of remaining Oskara who fought in the war against the Savoq years before Ethan was born. His strength and skill with his two handed war hammer was legend. He took an instant liking to the young prince even before Ethan began Oskara training. He taught him the history of battles and wars, believing that the best way to keep from repeating the atrocities of the past was to acknowledge and learn from them. Though the young Ethan begged to be taught in the use of weapons,

Blash kept the instruction to the skills of the mind, teaching the code of the Oskara and reading to him from texts written by both famed and obscure commanders of the past.

"It does me good to see you, boy!" The giant yelled as he strode up to Ethan. Nearby footmen looked shocked at his familiarity, but the mantle of royalty that separated Ethan from the majority of the population was not an issue between the two comrades. "Rumor of a fight has reached my ears, what say you?" Blash's guttural tones traced an unusual balance between Astarian and Goblin trade dialect. This came from his years as a child in the Western wilds where Astar and Goblin co-existed in an uneasy peace born out of necessity.

Swinging down, Ethan handed the reins of both horses to a stable boy who appeared, and clasped the large man's hand. "Friend, I may have a story to tell, but it will have to wait to be washed down with a pint of something cool." Blash glanced towards the bay and frowned. "Where is Kael?"

Ethan sighed; "Sadly, that is part of the tale." Turning towards the inner wall of the city, the two men walked in silence through the Focus Gate and through the markets full of the country people that brought their produce to be sold each day.

Only after his tankard was empty, did Ethan

speak again. They sat in the coolness of the Bracing Brew, an Inn and eatery set back from the main road and filled with dusty travelers.

He quickly told Blash what he had experienced on the plateau, doing his best to describe the dark creatures. Blash accompanied the story with grunts as he continued to pour his tankard filled with the brew of the Inn's namesake down his throat.

When Ethan finished his tale by describing the place he buried Kael, Blash leaned back and wiped a massive hand across his mouth. "I regret the passing of the brave lad, but his family will not want, I will see to it. To your words though, there have been other rumors. Murmurs of wraiths, shadows with claws in the border country. Men I have sent have not returned from the North. This I was to talk to you of once you returned."

Pulling out a leather map, Blash smoothed it on the table between them and pointed to the upper portion. It showed the border areas, and each village was marked. "I was choosing the men to go with me to investigate when you rode in. What say you to the joining of our merry band?"

"I would wish nothing else good friend," Ethan said, already formulating the best routes they should take. "I need to speak to my father, then I will be ready." Standing, he drained his cup and dropping enough coin to pay for the drink on the table, placed his hand on his chest in the Oskara sign of respect. Blash returned the salute and followed him out of the Inn. Once outside, he headed back towards the soldier's quarter as Ethan continued further into the city.

H<small>E TOOK HIS TIME</small>, soaking in the familiar views and taking time to talk to the people that filled the roadways and shops. He felt a connection to the common people, from a young age he began venturing out of the magnificent palace complex to explore the city. During those early years he made many friends during his excursions, among those his age as well as adults. The relationships grew as he made an effort to stay in communication with the populace whenever in the city.

The tall, thin spires of the palace came into view over the rooftops, towering above the landscape. The building of the palace had been ongoing since the city was founded four hundred years before, and was slowly expanding across the hilltop that capped the city. An iron bridge spanned a shallow moat that separated the palace grounds from the rest of the city. A fifty foot wall masked the view of the inner grounds, and as Ethan crossed the bridge, the familiar stark contrast greeted him. The crowded streets and gray stone buildings of the city seemed a world away as Ethan stepped into the luscious grass that marked the beginning of the palace gardens. The parks swept up the hill, dotted with towering trees of green, silver and scarlet, the ground not used as footpaths was covered in beautiful flowers. Crimson, emerald, pearl, orange, the colors soaked up the sunlight and let it out in glorious radiating swaths of beauty. The heady scent of the parks did much to lessen Ethan's exhaustion and stress, even as the miserly opulence grated against him. His family, for as long as he remembered, kept the gardens to themselves. The people of the city could only catch glimpses of the park. The legends of its beauty were fueled by the coming and going of great flocks of birds of paradise and the understanding that while it was close by, it was a world apart.

Ethan made his way up the paths to the palace entrance hidden in the wood nestled on the hilltop. Ornate scrollwork covered every surface, ivory and precious stones adorned the stone. As the economy of the city and the surrounding lands began to fall towards critical levels, the palace was alternatively updated and enlarged. This contrast fueled some minor unrest in the outlying population centers and small demonstrations in town squares were becoming commonplace. Further illustrating the chasm between royalty and citizens, there was a secret underground road that led from the palace to the woodlands east of the city for use by the royal family when the desire to hunt or otherwise wile away the days struck them. The road allowed them to move throughout the city without worry of encountering common folk. Now it was rare to ever see a Royal face to face, causing fact to become little more than rumor.

In the past the dissonance had grown into the ranks of the Royal Guard, responsible for the security of the palace and its parks. This unrest forced the ministries to dissolve the command. Rebuilt with semi-brainwashed soldiers, the command now lived their entire lives behind the walls of the palace grounds.

It all sickened Ethan. He was first a citizen and then a Royal, shunning the niceties of his station to work towards the betterment of his people. That was what drew him to the Oskara initially, the chance to lead and affect those around him. In his travels he saw the hurt and destitution throughout Astar. Farmlands were wallowing as drought and overuse of the soil persisted. The spreading of the swamp lands in the North, brought on by over logging of the surrounding forests, was also forcing the people to buy more supplies from the Goblins and the shipbuilders to the South. This necessitated the creation of trading roadways and their cost was taken directly from the towns along the routes. The situation was causing a growing number of people to move to the coastal areas and establish fishing villages to feed their families and be able to barter for other goods.

Ethan's ways created deep-seated resentments between him and his family as well as many city council leaders. That he left the palace grounds in his chosen life as a military man was grounds not only for his father to stop talking to him but also for the title of heir to be taken from him and given to his younger brother Eric.

As he stood at the entrance to his family home, he was struck by the lack of movement within the grounds. The usual abundance of traffic in and out of the palace was replaced by a stillness. The only people in sight being the guards at the moat and to either side of the ornate doors before him. Even they looked grim. If they could speak, he would have asked them about the change but the Royal Guard had sworn an oath of silence for the period of their enlistment. This had begun years before when Ethan's brothers, disliking a comment made by a guard in answer to their questioning took the issue before their father. This led to the implementation of the oath itself. It was a constant reminder of the power the royals held and it always caused Ethan piercing sadness and guilt when he saw the mute soldiers.

Returning the silent salute of the guards, he stepped through the ornate doorway. Just inside several servants scampered to take his muddied cloak and tried in vain to take his boots before he strode across the rich velvet carpets that covered every inch of the palace. His father had recently come down with gout, necessitating the soft, decadent surface. Ethan received no small pleasure at the exclamations of horror from nobles and their mistresses as he left a clear path of dirt towards the throne room.

6
PREPARATIONS TO LEAVE

OLIVER STOOD IN THE cavern far below the Citadel and tried to make his brain work. Until now he had been running on adrenaline with little more than murky goals to lead him. Panic now seized him. He was alone. All he knew and loved had been destroyed. His mind fought the truth of solitude, as it attempted to make up for the absence of others to talk to, to relate thoughts to.

Shaking with overwhelming fear he sank to the cold stone floor and hugged his knees, rocking back and forth. Tears streamed down his face, and if someone had been there to see, his young years were cruelly evident. The stone was wet beneath him by the time he unwrapped himself and stood on shaking legs. He slowly pulled the moonstone from his pocket and once again let the warmth flow through him until it faded completely, leaving the stone dark and cold. He sighed as he placed it back in his cloak and gathered the items on the table into a pile.

He took the book, the map, and the dagger. The weapon was now light in his hand as the power that had exploded from its pommel had left the simple metal oddly empty. Placing the items in the pockets of his cloak, he walked to the far side of the chamber where a natural hallway led into darkness. As there were no lights, Oliver used his glove again to project a floating orb before him. It continuously hovered just ahead as he moved through the passage. It wasn't long before he saw a hint of natural light and pressed the switch on his glove causing the orb to dissipate in a shower of sparks.

Hearing the sound of water crashing on rock, he headed around the next bend and found himself in a cave open to the surrounding lake. Rock floors turned to sand, leading to a small dilapidated dock. A small rowboat, in surprisingly good condition, rocked next to it. At least he would not have to build a raft to make his way off the island.

With the method of his passage across the water now dealt with, Oliver headed back through the rocky passage, through the cavern, and up the winding staircase into Magnus' rooms. He took a large leather pack from a closet and left the house, making his way through the strewn bodies and dried blood that covered the streets to the school housing area. He had a small room for late night study with some articles of clothing and he meant to begin his preparations there. The stench of decay was overpowering he used his cloak to block what he could.

Once there, he packed the few clothes stowed under the bed and the wool blanket that covered the mattress. Heading into the common areas, Oliver found the kitchen doors ajar and gathered what he believed would be enough food to last a week or two.

His pack nearly full, he left the room and made his way up the curved staircase of the tower that thrust skyward from the center of the school grounds. Reaching the platform that stood high above the Citadel's walls he looked out over the island that had been his entire life. His mind raced as he tried to focus on the familiar landmarks, attempting to maintain sanity as he stood in the silence. How had he survived? In some ways he wished he had not. At least then he would not be alone.

Shaking himself out of the daze, Oliver stepped to the golden doors of the tower and pushed them open. The Citadel observatory spread before him.

A massive rounded dome, it was filled with tables and shelves gathered around a large golden telescope that stretched towards a door in the curved ceiling high above. When opened, it allowed the telescope to be extended through the roof opening. The ceiling had a track on either side of the door, falling towards the floor in a half moon. This allowed the telescope to be elevated or moved along the track in a vertical manner to enable the finding and tracking of celestial bodies.

There were no signs that any Celestial Masters, as was their title, had been present at the time of the attack. Everything was as he remembered, cluttered in a regimented way. Oliver moved to the long tables on the far side of the room. These held the machines of the Seeker order. There were Solar capturing and reallocating devices, prototype weapons in some level of completion or another. Rows and rows of crystals of every color imaginable lined the walls. Copper piping and glass tubes combined into testing pods. In several of the tubes flashes of starlight circled lazily in an artificial vacuum.

He excitedly poured over it all. Oliver still required several years of training before he would acquire the status of Solari, a Seeker given the goal of enslaving Solar power. Because of this, he had not been allowed to see the majority of what was worked on here.

He could have stayed there for days. So much knowledge was before him and it took great effort to focus and search for the machine he had come for. It was in a corner covered in dust from obvious disuse. One of the first machines created to utilize the harnessed power of the sun, the Imbuer was a mass of copper coils and wire connections. Framed in oak, it was topped by a box made entirely of gray crystal. Its purpose was to transfer solar energy from the sun into inanimate objects. His moonstone had been infused with energy a year ago. A student's use of the Imbuer was highly restricted and only allowed for educational purposes when under direct supervision.

Seekers in the decades before had discovered a slight healing element when they fused solar energy into pure onyx crystal. While not having much effect against grave illness or severe injury, there was a slight lessening of negative effects and an improvement in morale and nerves when used. Seekers officially called the stones "beacons of light" as they would lift the spirits in time of darkness. Their common name was moonstone.

Oliver's moonstone required a refill of this energy. He had a rudimentary understanding of the machines from his studies and now worked his way through the tables until he came across a long pipe, able to flex on hinged grooves. One end wound through the equipment and attached to a large tank made of yellow crystal. The tank surface glowed softly, a sign that solar energy was present. Oliver hooked the opposite end of the pipe to an opening on the Imbuer's box and released a valve. Soundlessly, the energy quickly filled the small box, bringing the glow with it.

Seconds later he returned the valve to its place and placed his stone on a small lead tray in the center of the the Imbuer. He then connected the copper coils to the box using the excess of wire and stepped back. The coils were used to transfer the energy from the energy source to any object placed on the tray by way of induction heating. The lead tray focused the small magnetic field needed to pull the energy into the stone. Sparks began to fly as the energy boiled out of the box and along the coils, revolving again and again around the stone until it seemed to be encased in silvery liquid. A final flash and cascade of sparks erupted as energy was drawn into the black crystal and the glow from the box faded, depleted.

He picked up the energized moonstone and dropped it in a pocket, then repeated the entire process until he had four more of the energized stones. He removed his cloak in order to unstrap his glove and the leather harness carried on his shoulders. The two were linked by a transparent tube of flexible crystal and allowed the flow of energy from the shoulder mounted container to the glove's metal leads when the thumb studs were pressed. The narrow tank was sectioned into three separate containers for the different types of energy that corresponded to the different studs.

Oliver filled the first container with the same energy used in the moonstone. The second came from an identical reservoir on a separate table that glowed a muted silver. This was moonlight, refined by running it through the purer sun energy several times to bring out its slightly more latent energy. This was the source of the orb he had called forth before. The third container he filled with a liquid substance made from melting fallen stars and then thinning the resulting substance with quicksilver. This was the most rare and costly of the three as it had been a decade since the last starfall. The shield he had used when the Citadel was attacked had been formed of this.

A little heavier, and much steadier, Oliver walked through the observatory looking for anything else useful that he would be able to carry with him. He found two small pouches of solar dust that could melt through any known metal and another shoulderpack that matched his and filled its containers as well. Standing next to the telescope as he prepared to leave, he wished he knew how to operate it to see what so many had seen before him. Sighing, he left the room and took the tower stairs two at a time until he reached the cobbled roadway. He didn't notice when the notebook he had taken from the chest fell from his cloak and landed in the doorway.

As Oliver left the school grounds he suddenly realized that he had no standard weapons or tools for a journey of any kind. He ran towards the dockyards and searched through the warehouses until he found two rolls of fishing line and several hooks as well as a sturdy oak staff. As he looked around for a weapon of some kind he remembered the sword that he had picked up earlier and left inside the Citadel council room. He shook his head as a rueful grin spread across his face at the thought of his wielding a warrior's weapon; he would make do with the dagger from the chest.

7
FATHER AND SON

As he waited for permission to enter, Ethan leaned against the tapestries hanging outside the throne room and tried to prepare himself for the audience. He tried to picture his father as the invalid that people had been whispering of in recent times. He could only see the strong arrogant features and broad shoulders of the sportsman king that he had grown up with.

The change, when he entered the throne room, frightened him. His father was a thin relic of what had been, a wasted face atop a bony torso. A golden staff, most likely used to support him, leaned against the throne.

As he saw his eldest son, a look of tired relief flitted across Luitger's face but was quickly replaced by the cold detachment that Ethan knew so well. A withered hand beckoned, though the king remained in repose.

Ethan moved towards the throne and bowed, giving the greeting of royalty; "My Sovereign, may your strength never waver." When the king nodded in reply, Ethan stepped back and began to lay out his tale. He quickly told the king of his experience in the wastelands and of the rumors from the North. He ended by describing the valiant effort of his fallen comrade and what he was putting in place to support the grieving family.

The king accepted the news with a blank look, as he waved his hand in a dismissive gesture. His voice rasped, slightly louder than a whisper, and his eyes remained unfocused. "You, of all in this land are adept at weaving false tales. Even to the point that a man would follow you into death."

Startled and confused, Ethan stepped closer and knelt just in front of the throne. "My loyalty lies here, my Sovereign. When have I been known to brings lies?"

A fit of coughing shook the once strong shoulders as Luitger bent forward. "My spies have been witness to them! How dare you question my word!" Drawing in rattling breaths the king sank back into the throne, rage competing with weariness. "You, my ingrate son, have brought nothing but shame to me. Try as you may to spread your name and exploits by telling stories, you will remain a castoff."

"My Lord," Ethan began through clenched teeth, "If what I bring is truth, what then? Will you not do anything to protect the innocent people of our nation?"

"Innocent? Is there such a thing anymore? My counsel has been full of what these *innocents* are doing, within my city and without!" The king straightened as he continued. "Prices fall and fields go fallow. Killings are commonplace, what is this but in answer to the guilt that covers MY people?"

Bowing his head to hide his rage, Ethan stood. "My king, I fear for this land. With this fear comes responsibility to do what I can to work against evil and wrongdoing. With your permission I will go and investigate the rumors in the North. If I find nothing I will not speak of them again."

"Get out of my sight and go where you will!" Luitger raged before falling back with a fit of coughing as servants hurried to bring drink. He did not look at Ethan again.

E THAN SEETHED AS HE nearly ran from the throne room. The unlucky nobles that did not make way were knocked from their feet as he tore from the palace. Those that saw his eyes blanched at the fury within.

He made the long walk to the tavern, where he had separated from Blash, in silence. He could not understand the change that had come over his father. The king had once truly loved his people and had worked to better their lives. What lies had he began to listen to, and more importantly, who was the author of them?

He found Blash sitting at a large table with two soldiers he recognized. Waving away the questions that looked ready to gush from Blash's lips, Ethan sat and beckoned to the proprietor for drink. "We have our permission to investigate the rumors. We leave at dawn."

Blash nodded his satisfaction and, turned to address the others. "We were just going over the numbers of men and supplies needed for the excursion and then will be ready. Two score will be the size of our party, allowing faster movement." The seated Oskara knights Rekin and Rylr, young brothers who had been apprenticed under Blash and Ethan, voiced their agreement and began to debate the necessary equipment.

Before they could continue, Ethan stood, drained the flagon handed to him and prepared to leave. "I have need of sleep. Thank you for your support in this. You can find me at the soldier quarters if necessary." After giving the Oskara salute he made his way to the long building that housed the majority of Astar Footmen that were currently activated. When he found an open bed he all but fell onto it and was asleep within moments.

8
STEELFORGE

OLIVER STOOD AT THE Citadel's main entrance that overlooked the small vegetable gardens and the docks beyond. The once majestic white marble walls were now streaked with ash and the gold plated gates hung askew, battered and broken. Silent tears flowed freely as he drank in what had once been home. It was now tainted by the evil that destroyed it, by the stench of death, and by the memory of lost happiness.

Shouldering the gear he had collected, Oliver walked through the desolate streets and made his way down the winding stairs to the cavern. When he arrived at the dilapidated dock once again, he stowed the gear in the boat and untied the mooring rope. Pulling on the oars, he wrestled the small craft through the narrow cleft and out onto the wide lake. Birds nesting in the rocks above burst from their roosts shrieking their displeasure at his unexpected appearance.

Without looking back, he navigated to the shoreline near the old trading post that was used as shelter for travelers and the few traders that came to the Citadel. A narrow road ran north through the dilapidated buildings and on into the plains. As he landed and began to collect his gear Oliver allowed himself a quick glance back at the island. The image burned into his memory. A shattered hulk, the Citadel lay blackened and still smoking, surrounded by the masts and rigging of sunken ships. Choking back tears, Oliver turned to the road and headed North.

He was unsure of where he was to go, other than towards the now setting sun and slightly north. He hoped that he would come across some kind of civilization, a place where he might find some sort of guidance. He followed the gently sloping roadway as it began to bend to the Northwest, towards the Goblin lands in the Stony Hills and the mountains beyond. The way was easy, as the road led through the knee high grasses of endless green fields. The scents of spring growth and flowers in the air buoyed his spirits.

As the sun began to fall below the distant mountains, Oliver came upon the first sign of life. A small stone cottage surrounded by a vegetable garden came into view as he made his way through the sparse woods that marked the Western border of the open lands. A laughing goblin-child suddenly ran from behind the structure, and pulled up short as it saw him. A young she-goblin followed the child and quickly motioned for it to come to her as she met Oliver's gaze.

He had only seen a few Goblins in his life, and those were the traveling tradesmen that came to Sun Fire to barter for goods. He tried not to stare at the blunt faces and squat forms of the two. They had gray, pale skin and long arms that ended in thick hands with only four fingers. The woman wore a simple dress of pliable leather. Thick braids of black hair fell to her knees.

He awkwardly bent his head in a sign of respect and said hello. The goblin returned the nod and surprised Oliver by speaking in clear Astarian. "Where are you traveling to and who may you be?"

He hesitated a moment then replied. "I am a Seeker, Oliver is my name and I am heading Northwest. Is there a village nearby where I could find a place to stay the night?"

"But a few miles further up the main road is our capital city of Steelforge where you are sure to find something. I am sorry, I do not mean to pry but we do not see the large folk hardly at all these days."

Oliver admitted with a smile, "No apology is necessary. I am unaccustomed to traveling outside my home and I thank you for your help."

He bowed his farewell as he left the goblins and continued into the woods. A quiet tinkle of laughter from the younger goblin followed him, reddening his face. The land began to rise, marking the foothills that were the traditional home of the Goblin race. He began to tire, unused to the travel and weight of his gear. His legs and back burned and he hoped the goblin had been correct.

Shortly after, the small dirt path he had been following widened into a sizable cobbled road and the muted sounds of activity filtered through the trees. He came up over a rise in the road and the city was suddenly spread before him.

Low buildings were strung along the road and goblin folk hurried here and there as they finished their day's work. The city was arrayed on a steep slope that ended at a towering rock cliff. A market filled the large courtyard at the center of the city. Fresh produce and racks upon racks of dried and raw fish were being covered and stored for the next day. Oliver was barely given a second glance as he walked through the markets. As he was more than a head taller than those around him it was easy to navigate the winding street and the market stalls.

He asked a shopkeeper installing a leather cover on his produce stall where the nearest inn might be. The shopkeeper turned, irritated at the interruption. On seeing the young human before him, he sighed and pointed further up the road. "There be a decent kind o' place not a hundred feet of here, my boy." He added with a grating chuckle; "Though the beds may be a mite short."

Oliver thanked him and kept moving through the deepening twilight. Within moments he caught sight of the well-lit inn. He stooped to enter the low building and found himself in a long open room with doors along the far wall. A wizened old she-goblin made her way to the small table that stood near the door. "Welcome to Steelforge. You want a room, young giant?" she asked with a smile.

Blushing, Oliver replied, "I have need of a place to rest for the night. I have payment."

"By all means, you may stay and payment will be gratefully taken. I must apologize for the shortness of the beds though."

"Believe me, I would be able to sleep on the dirt itself." Oliver said with a tired grin. Inwardly he felt shame at his lack of knowledge of their language as everyone he had spoken with knew his so well.

The old she-goblin led him to one of the many doors and handed him a key. "Sleep well and deep, young sir. Food will be provided when you wake."

Oliver mumbled his thanks as he bent through the door and placed his pack down inside the room. He took off his cloak, washed his face with water from a bowl set on a low table and then sank onto the bed. Though he had to curl up to keep from hanging off, the day's travels made it seem the most comfortable bed he had ever slept in.

HE AWOKE TO KNOCKING on his door. Rubbing his eyes, he opened it to find three Goblin soldiers in full plate armor, two with axes in hand. The lead goblin scowled and said, "When word of your arrival came we were sent to bring you to the internal city. Please gather your belongings and come with us."

Confused and frightened, Oliver did as they asked, following the soldiers from the inn as the owner watched with a worried frown. As he went he wondered what they meant by an internal city.

Dawn was just casting its hazy light as he was led deeper into the city. As they walked through the quiet streets, the only other folk they came across were traders loading carts for their day's journey and lone city watchmen making their un-hurried rounds.

The road got steeper as they walked and Oliver began to pant from the effort of keeping the quick pace of his custodians. This surprised him as his legs were a good foot longer. They passed through a broad gate, sentinels on either side standing guard in silence. The houses on either side dis-appeared but the road continued up to the rocky hillside until they came to the cliff face. It seemed to be an unbroken surface but the lead goblin sud-denly disappeared into it. Oliver was led into the mouth of a cave hidden from without by a vine-like growth. Once inside he stood and stared at the sight before him.

The underground city was like nothing like he had ever seen. In the place of the simple roads and shops and homes outside, was a maze of rail sys-tems. The rails rose and fell in the darkness of the enormous cavern to connect countless platforms on which goblins went about morning activities. Small and large cart-like vehicles swayed and jolt-ed along the sinuous cables and rails in dizzying numbers. The cavern was lit by an endless network of what appeared to be long, clear tubes flowing with a luminescent liquid of glowing amber. Then there were the sounds that echoed throughout the chamber. The clanking of gears and hissing of steam pumps blanketed the chamber in a chorus of machinery.

He couldn't make out the bottom of the chasm as it burrowed far into the darkness. A wave of dizziness swept through him as he teetered on the shelf of stone that made up the entrance. A swaying cart sped towards them, coming to an abrupt stop before them.

Motioned forward, Oliver gingerly stepped into the swaying transport and took the offered seat on a low bench bolted to the floor. His keepers joined him and the leader spoke a word in their native tongue to the cart's pilot, a young male goblin. In answer the pilot turned a wheel and pulled a long lever, sending the cart racing back down the track and deep into the city below.

9
INVESTIGATION

THE MORNING MISTS WERE still heavy when Ethan and his mounted command clattered across the drawbridge. He had woken refreshed and met with Blash for final preparations before leaving the city.

He placed Rylr in the lead position and he now held back, riding alongside Blash. They traveled northwest all morning, stopping in the small riverside town of Newson to water their horses and inquire whether signs of trouble had been witnessed. Refreshed and with no new information, they forded the Foar River and continued on the main road through country that began to roughen and crack. Ravines bracketed the roadways and thorns fought small trees for dominance. Known as the highlands, the area was used mainly for hunting the wild boar that roamed there. Passing through the highlands they entered the Havan

Forest where a small population ran wood mills that were scattered throughout the area. These mills were in high demand due to the extremely hard wood of the trees found only in this forest.

They rode through two more villages before evening fell, each with the same outcome. No one had heard of the rumors, though many had been happy to share whatever gossip they had with the soldiers.

Ethan pushed his men into the night, sticking to the main roads when possible to keep their horse's footing. It was near midnight when he called a halt at the northeast edge of the forest near the entrance to Helk Gorge. The group quickly set up camp, caring for the horses and preparing food. Rekin set up a watch of two footmen on rotating shifts before joining the other leaders.

Blash was just sayin, "To go much farther would be to walk into the sea. I know of a few more villages within a few hours ride that are the northernmost part of the country."

Nodding, Rekin added, "I know of one of the three as my brother and I have cousins there." He grinned. "The nearby fishing is good too."

"I would like nothing more than to put these rumors to rest and find out if that statement is completely valid." Ethan replied. "Until then, stay vigilant. Get some rest, we leave at dawn."

It took no more than an hour to reach the village of Krayal. They saw the smoke rising over the trees before they broke through the surrounding wood. The village hugged the coast, buildings spread over the open ground and jutted out over the sea on stilted platforms. Or at least they had in the recent past. Even the dirt was scorched from a fire that still smoldered in places.

As he motioned for his men to dismount and spread out, Ethan moved into the village. The first sign of the inhabitants was a foot. Suspended on a rack used to dry fish, the appendage appeared to have been torn from its owner and tossed aside. Ethan used his cloak to cover his nose from the rising stench that began to enfold him and continued on to look for the rest of the body. He found it mere feet away, legs missing, features mutilated.

Bending down, Ethan touched the forehead of the body and said a quick blessing before moving on. He listened to the calls of his men as they reported additional bodies. Among the buildings the ground was littered with shredded corpses. Villagers lay among the day's catch, rotting fish lying amid the men and women. Something strong and crazed must have done this, Ethan thought, trying to fit the injuries with any predator he knew.

With a chill he settled on the only predator large and cruel enough in his experience. Man or something that thought much like them. Only men could think to brutalize others in this way and yet leave the bodies uneaten. But what of the rumors and the creatures he had seen in the High Plains? Could they be here in the North as well? It would fit, the injuries and the heartlessness suited the darting, ripping shadows.

A cry from his right made Ethan start. He charged through the broken and smoking ruins until he came upon a small knot of his men. They huddled around the small body of a boy just about to reach manhood. Rylr held the body, rocking it back and forth as tears rolled down his face. Rekin ran to Ethan's side and cried out in horror. "Not Rayek too!" Turning to Ethan he blurted, "He was the son of our cousin. We stayed at his house and played with this boy. He taught us to fish." Tears threatened to fall but Rekin forced them back. "I found his parents on the docks, torn apart like the others."

Ethan gripped his shoulder and promised. "I will not rest until we find who or what did this. We will have our vengeance."

Ethan called out to Blash as he made his way

to the docks, meeting the big man on his way. "We must bury these people. We will not leave until they are laid to rest and the proper blessing has been spoken."

Blash nodded somberly. "Aye it will be as you say. I fear I wish that death had taken me prior to being witness to such a thing."

He moved away, shouting orders to the surrounding soldiers. Ethan remained and looked out at the waves gently cresting past the docks, tears for the dead in his eyes.

10
THE COUNCIL

A WEEK LATER, ETHAN BURST into the Chamber of Honor with eyes blazing. He shoved past several councilmen to reach the head of the Speaker's Table and pounded his mailed fist into the wood with such force that a split ran the length of the surface with a loud crack. Silence quickly filled the room. All eyes turned towards him, few without anger at the intrusion. The High Speaker, Councilman Morcant, began to speak in protest but Ethan cut him off with a glare that caused Morcant to take a step back. "I am here to take what is due!" he thundered. "I will take what is due the people who fell without aid, without hope, as you, the council of Astar, debated for the sake of hearing your own voices!"

A few councilmen began to move towards to the doors but stopped short when they saw four of Ethan's men barring the way, their hands near a wide assortment of weapons.

Ethan continued, "As you whittled away the days in insidious back stabbings and ignorant talk, men, women and children have been slain. Under your watch have the people been exposed to danger and death." Slowing his speech, he began to speak more quietly. "I have just come from the border town of Krayal, all that was left of the inhabitants were the tattered remnants of bodies, thrown as if by a great wind. Once we completed our initial investigation, I sent scouts to you with a full report and a request for additional soldiers. I then bid half my command to secure the area surrounding the village and await word from you and led the remainder to the town of Veyris. It had not been harmed and we checked on four more over the next three days. Once satisfied, we moved back to Krayal and regrouped with my men there. I was confused at the lack of additional troops and asked after my scouts with no reply. We immediately moved out, in two separate groups this time, one South, the other North along the coast. I left a few men to wait at Krayal for the requested support and sent another two scouts to this council."

Ethan paused to regain his breath before resuming, his glare holding the room in rapt silence. "Both the command I led and the other with Blash in the lead, witnessed the same fate. Town after town, village after village, all within a full day's travel was burning. Yes, even the ones we had just visited! It was as it had been at Krayal. A menace has breached the gates of our fair country, an unspeakable evil. Creatures strong enough to tear limb from limb yet with a tactical understanding that enabled them to keep my force from locating and cornering them."

Quickly interjecting, Speaker Morcant exclaimed "You cannot place blame on us, this is the first we have heard such things! Your men were never brought before us."

Seething, Ethan rattled the table with another blow, "You lie! As I passed through the city, even this council's offices, I heard the whispers, saw the fear in the people's eyes. Even now I recognize the look of resignation on the faces in this hall, as I have put to death the rumor and made it a living thing, something we must combat. If only I had been heard when I first spoke of the dark creatures in the High Plains!"

"And what of my scouts that came to this council with reports from my foray to the borderlands? I come back to find them discredited and put behind bars, because to acknowledge them would have forced you to act! Forced you to work through the heavy decisions required for a proper and timely response. If you had done what you have been established to do in the absence of Royal command, men, women and children who are dead would still be alive, protected by our great and numerous armies."

"Your political games have had grave implications. You will be held accountable on my word as a Royal Son!"

Ethan turned and swept through the gathered men, locking his dark gaze with any brave enough to match it on his way to the exit. He signaled his men to follow as he moved quickly from the building. Shouts rang out in the chamber behind him, and he knew he did not have much time before word of his outburst reached his father.

Blash met him with a grin at the fountain that fronted the council chambers. "Even these old ears be hearing what went on inside, friend! I only wish to have seen the faces, but I fear that my fists would have found their way to an overabundance of throats!"

Ethan chuckled and replied with a rueful look on his face, "I may have been a mite harsh on the poor men that watch over us." He clapped the big man on his shoulder as they continued away from the government grounds. "Mayhap in another life

I would have cared, those toothless snakes deserve worse!"

His men grunted in hearty agreement.

11
POWER PLAY

Shortly after ethan left the council, Councilman Morcant stalked through the cavernous halls towards his office in the rear of the building. Deep in thought, he tried to make sense of what he had heard. No word had reached him through his spies of the events laid out by the prince. He did not like being in the dark and he hated being shamed in public, especially by the errant son of a feeble king. Anger colored his normally pale face.

He was not an attractive man, a stringy goatee hung from a thin hollow face and long, straight white hair tumbled past his shoulders. His rare smiles revealed a mouthful of rotten teeth. Shaggy brows overshadowed his piercing dark eyes. Morcant was not a beloved personality and if he had ever cared about what others thought of him, those days were far behind. Only the draw of power meant anything to him now and he found his startling appearance useful during negotiations.

Reaching his doors, he pushed them open and knocked his secretary sprawling to the floor, scrolls and books flying. With a snarl, Morcant kicked at the prostrate form as he swept past. His servant had many uses that were critical to his plans, but he bore no love for the misshapen creature. He still did not know where "it" had come from or even what "it" was. During his early career Morcant had been required to travel across Astar lands, inspecting villages and gathering intelligence. It was during one of these excursions that he had been accosted by men with ideas of robbery and worse. But as he lay huddled on the muddy road waiting for further blows to fall, a choking scream had echoed across the surrounding fields. He and his attackers had been frozen at the sound.

The inhuman scream wavered as its strength grew, slicing through Morcant's brain with searing pain and blacking out his sight. The sound somehow worked its way into the heads of the men and caused certain nerve connections to overload, resulting in a form of brain failure. Luckily for Morcant, the sound was directional, able to be rudimentary aimed so that the brunt of its effects hit only his attackers. His eyesight was all that had been affected and it took a few hours to return.

During that time he crept off the road and sat shivering in fear, listening as the human screams of his attackers slowly faded as their brains shut down.

The silence, when it fell, was much worse than the screams and his mind began to form the creature that had uttered the cry. A dark, blurred deformed thing with red eyes and hissing breath that smelled of sulfur. He was shocked when he realized his eyesight had returned and the thing crouched before him was not a figment of his imagination. It was nearly enough to push him into unconsciousness.

When he finally understood that he was not in danger he began to inspect the creature. Vaguely man shaped and draped in scraps of stained clothing it looked almost pitiful. In the large red eyes he recognized terror and a need he was surprised to understand; a need to be connected to power, to feel sustained and protected by it, to be able to map out one's own life.

From then on the creature, whom Morcant called Fell, never left his side, becoming the most valuable servant he had known. Fell had been disguised in padded clothing and passed off as a hunchbacked mix of goblin and man, allowing it the ability to operate in public as Morcant's spymaster. In this, the creature had no equal. Drawing those with darkness in their hearts as a fly to honey, Fell built a network that spanned the known lands. This allowed Morcant to keep apprised of key events so that he could manipulate outcomes at will to benefit his own plans.

Now Morcant stalked around his office, throwing anything he could get his long, bony fingers on at Fell as the creature twisted on the floor, small cries emitting from the hooded figure. Failure and shame were not allowed to happen! Seething, he yelled at Fell, berating and questioning his spymaster's ability to gather information.

He paused for breath and collapsed into his high backed chair and pulled at his goatee. His anger dissipated quickly, and Fell, noticing, stood and filled a goblet with wine for its master. Sighing, Morcant spoke, "I grow tired, Fell. Tired of waiting, counting on weaker minds to maintain control. I do not blame you entirely as the movements of this princeling are erratic at best. We are too close to be affected by such developments. The end is in sight."

Struggling for the right words, as it had taken Fell years to learn the human tongue, his minion replied, "Master is correct in this, master will succeed as he always has. Fell must do better to be worthy of the power to come."

Smiling in response, Morcant placed a hand on Fell's shoulder and stood, draining the goblet. "I will go to the King and further our cause. Send spies to the affected villages that the prince spoke of and have them searched for survivors. If any are found have them brought to me here."

He strode to the back of his office and swept aside the heavy tapestry that hid a bolted iron door. With a key taken from his robes, Morcant opened the door and made his way along the claustrophobic hallway that led downward at a slight angle.

In the maze of tunnels underneath the city, he had found those that ran close to the palace years ago. He had hired engineers to create connecting pathways so that he could come and go as he pleased. He despised walking across the palace bridge like a common noble and instead chose the more authoritarian method of showing up in the King's personal wing of the palace at times of his choosing. Only he and Fell truly understood the tunnel system, as the engineers had been killed on completion of their work. Fell still kept trophies of the kills in his burrow far below the city.

Morcant finally reached the door he needed and opened it silently on oiled leather hinges. He was in the dark looking out into a long hall. The back of a towering throne sat just ahead. An arm holding up a heavy head was all he could see of Astar's current ruler.

12
TO MEET A RULER

Oliver lost count of the platforms they passed before the swaying cart slowed. Ahead the overhead lights grew in size, brightening the area with an unnatural glare. For the third time he tried to get some information on what was going on. "Sirs, where are we going? Have I done something wrong?"

Stony, expressionless faces looked through him and no reply was forthcoming. Oliver sighed, slumped back in his seat and watched a large golden hued wall and massive gate creep into view as they slowed. They came to a stop on what seemed to be the bottom of the chasm, a flat stony surface covered in rock dust. Here, the rail line ended.

A cheerful looking goblin strolled up and engaged the cart's braking system before looking the occupants over. "Welcome be to you young friend." He said to Oliver. "What brings you to the

'Floor of the Sea' as we call it?"

Before Oliver could reply one of the armored goblins spoke sharply in their grating language and the rail worker quickly backed away, his cheerful look fading into something closer to apprehension.

Oliver was led to the large metal door. Two torches stood on either side of an inscribed plate embedded in the wall. Just above the plate hung a rope. The leader of the soldiers reached up and pulled hard on the rope once and stepped back to join the other two soldiers. Nothing happened at first, then a low rumble of sound came from behind the wall and then silence once again.

Oliver started when the gate began to open. Slowly, the heavy door swung on silent hinges, opening into darkness. As the group moved through the gateway, small pinpricks of light flamed to life. Candles, hundreds of candles standing on narrow stone pillars, lit the space beyond the wall. Behind each candle stood a young goblin, alternating male and female. They were spaced every ten or so paces.

The illuminated area showed that they were moving through a cleft in the cliff face, winding as it followed the natural curves of the rock. A cold draft of air made Oliver shiver as they walked. The silence was just about to make him crazy when the trail widened and the line of candles ceased.

Ahead was a solid wall of darkness. The soldiers halted and stood quietly. Oliver waited with them, shivering in the subterranean cold, glancing at the solemn candle bearers around them.

The sudden boom of a drum shattered the silence as more candles flared to life. Oliver drew his breath in sharply. The group stood at the entrance to a long natural cavern, not unlike the one underneath Sun Fire Citadel. The floor was not smooth, jagged rock shot up in all directions, making the room look as if a giant mouth had opened. At the far side of the cavern a score or more goblins stood gathered around a single goblin seated on what appeared to be a throne. The hall was formed out of living rock, the throne itself little more than a shelf of stone bordered on each side by two round boulders.

Waved forward by another armored goblin that stood next to the throne, Oliver's group crossed the distance between the entrance and the rough dais. The three goblins that had brought him knelt on one knee, plate armor folding smoothly as they moved. Oliver quickly did likewise, returning to stand upright with the guards. Only then did he meet the eyes of the goblin sitting on the throne.

He was old, not old like Oliver understood, more ancient than any human he had seen. He seemed a part of the stone chair that held him. The gray skin was creased and cracked, the features loose. His hair was but wisps of white strands that stuck out of the simple iron circlet on his brow. The eyes were different. Alive, even young, they pierced through Oliver and made him lower his gaze and redden in shyness.

"Welcome to the Deep Fallows young human." The voice grated like millstones. "I am Bosgar, leader of the Goblin race. It is my great honor to meet you. I had grown worried I may not last until this day."

Oliver stumbled through his reply. "Good sir, it is I who should be honored. Is there something that I have done wrong?"

The room erupted in coarse laughter, the sound reverberating off the rock walls as even the candle bearers joined in. "Nay, tall one! You have done nothing wrong and I am sorry for the secrecy of your journey here. My captain enjoys putting fear into outsiders in general and he had to be talked into allowing you this deep." Bosgar pointed with a smile to the leader of the three goblins that had escorted Oliver.

With a hearty bellow of laughter the accused

turned to Oliver and embraced him, squeezing the breath out of him. "You be a right solemn human, and it did me good to see you not quake in your boots!"

Released, Oliver stood in relieved confusion, a smile breaking out as the laughter and conversation continued unabated. The goblin leader raised a hand above his head and all fell silent. "Now as to why you are here, we must talk. We do not allow humans access to this place for sport. My scouts have reported that the Citadel called Sun Fire is destroyed and that you were the only one seen leaving the island." At Oliver's startled look Bosgar raised his hand reassuringly. "They followed you to protect you until you could come before me. I have need of understanding what danger is on our threshold. I understand loved ones may have perished, but please tell us what transpired on that dark island as time may be of great importance."

Oliver spoke haltingly. "Sir, it is as you say, I am from Sun Fire. I had never left until yesterday." Bosgar bade him and the others nearby take seats and then nodded to Oliver to continue. Oliver then spoke of what he had seen, relating the events as best he could remember, hiding only the details of the cavern and its secrets. Throughout his tale the goblins looked at one another and made whispered comments back and forth.

When Oliver finished his story, the goblin Leader stood and clasped his arms with an iron grip. "Child, you will be from this day, a part of my people, a son of a lost island. We weep with you in your loss and rejoice in your life. You are welcome to stay here and need only ask for anything."

Touched deeply, Oliver wiped away a tear threatening to escape. "Thank you, honored sir. I know now, the world does your people unjustly in their reports. I can find no words to thank you and have nothing with which to repay your generosity."

"Who among us said anything of repayment!" barked Bosgar. "Your repayment to us is to accept our help with a free heart. That is all we wish."

Oliver was humbled and could not stop the tears that streamed down his face. He took a steadying breath, then remembered his quest. "I do have a request, though I am loath to ask it."

Bosgar answered quietly but firmly, "It will be seen as an affront to our people if you hold your need back from us."

Oliver bowed his head and continued, "I am looking for a way to the mountains across the Beryl Sea. Are there any among your people who can give me guidance before I must continue my journey?"

As he mentioned the mountains, he saw the surrounding goblins freeze with startled looks on their stony faces. "What do you have to do in the Shadowmyst mountains my good friend?" The guard captain slowly asked.

"Darrin" Bosgar intoned. "The asking is not a requirement I hold to. This boy has asked our help, we shall give it." Beckoning a goblin dressed in a leather robe of some kind to his side, Bosgar whispered something to him. The goblin bowed once and quickly moved out of sight.

"I ask your forgiveness for bringing you here under darkness and so quickly. We cannot trust the eyes that linger where they should not in the sunlit world." Darrin said softly as the gathering began to talk amongst themselves.

Oliver replied quickly. "Forgiveness is granted and your actions are understandable. Do not think on it further."

As Darrin grunted his satisfaction the drum boomed again. All the goblins, along with Oliver turned towards the entrance. Two sturdy goblins strode in and made their way to the group. They bowed their respect to Bosgar before the lead goblin spoke. "Honored father, I and your younger son are at your command. We are understanding that a human has been welcomed." He nodded his head in deference to Oliver. "We stand ready to fulfill the need that was brought before you."

Bosgar clapped his massive hands together, pleased. "Well met, my sons! Make our people proud by your actions in this." He turned to Oliver and spoke, "Young sir, these are the two that will guide you on your journey to the Shadowmyst mountains. My eldest is Farl, the younger, Skrit. Our hope is that they will fulfill your need. But now!" He nearly shoved Oliver towards an opening in the rock wall to the side of the throne. "We feast on the bounty that comes from the ground and the sea!"

As they went, Oliver, still wary and confused, asked Darrin, "Why are your people helping me? I am unknown to them, yet they provide guidance and protection as if my dealings are their own."

Hurrying Oliver to keep up with the jovial procession, Darrin replied with a quick, "Ah lad, that be a tale for another time and from another's lips. It be time to empty your mind and fill your belly!"

13
BANISHMENT

ETHAN PACED IN FRONT of the doors to the throne room, once again forced to wait. He had left Blash the task of putting together men and supplies for a larger expedition to weed out the unseen enemy in the North. The brothers Rekin and Rylr had left the city to gather those men loyal to Ethan who had been sent home for the Spring harvests.

The door finally opened and he strode quickly into the shadowy hall. He instantly noticed the addition of royal guardsmen, a full score lined the walls. His father remained seated as before and was in conversation with a tall robed figure. Bowing his respect of the office if not the man, Ethan moved to stand below the throne.

The robed man turned at his approach and he recognized the thin face and scowl of Councilman Morcant. A sneer endeavored to pull the thin lips as he gave a slight bow to the prince. The three remained motionless for long seconds. Suddenly, the King bent forward and held out his gnarled hand for Ethan to take. Ethan, surprised by the gesture, gripped the hand.

Using Ethan as support, Luitger pulled his shaking form up and stood glaring at his son, dark brows drawn together. "You dare to stand before me! My traitor of a son, your depravity shames me in my old age!" Casting away Ethan's hand he bellowed, "You are no longer a son of mine! Go back to the hell you came from."

Ethan tried to speak, "My lord, I am unfairly accu…" The King interrupted him by spitting in his face. Wiping the wetness away, Ethan felt a twinge of fear and stepped back a couple paces as he glanced around him. The guards had moved closer, hands to weapons.

Shaking his head, Luitger turned and accepted the proffered staff from Morcant. "You are not of this family any longer, never return." So saying the King slowly left the room, helped by servants. Ethan stood as if turned to ice and watched his father leave. It was over, the finality and suddenness of it took his breath. He was no longer the son of a king, nor a son at all. He steeled himself against the feelings of pain and confusion that rattled through him.

Breaking through his thoughts, Morcant whispered, "How did this happen I wonder?" He paused, locking eyes with Ethan. "I may know something of it." Ethan moved to shake what the man knew out of him, but was brought up short by the hafts of spears barring his way. The guards now stood in a close ring around him, blank looks on their faces as they held weapons at the ready.

Cackling, Morcant stepped forward and took his seat on the throne. The impudence of the act made Ethan want to scream. "How dare you, dog of a man! You are a traitor tenfold for taking that seat!

Clasping his bony fingers before him, Morcant spoke slowly. "I have been in control of he who sits on this throne for many years, why should I not see how it feels? You, a simple commoner, will never feel the power I wield."

"I knew something was not right with the King," Ethan spat out. "That someone must have had his ear. Now I know the culprit, you devious snake."

The thin man continued with a dismissive gesture, "Do you wish to know what sent your late-father tottering over the edge in his feelings for you? Ahh, it was beautiful. I fostered in your father a fear that everything you said was twisted and unable to be trusted. Slowly I built on this idea over many months. Your many journeys facilitated the process and the King began to doubt the son who had already caused so much pain by throwing away the mantle of royalty. You made it easy with your tall tales, of which I have moderate confidence were in themselves true. The truth said with a word added or taken here or there stretches what is believed until anything is possible in the mind of the one receiving the information."

Pausing, Morcant waved a servant over and took the small object he offered. "After I listened to your boyish tirade before the council, it gave me an idea. I sent my favorite spy to follow the trail you had spoken of. To each of the destroyed villages did he go. Using the men he had with him, he made it look as if an errant band of horse mounted soldiers had done the deed." He unwrapped the packet and let Ethan see, bits of pendant and several arrowheads lay there. Along with the head of a small child.

Reeling in horror, Ethan clenched every muscle in his body as his eyes darted around him, looking for any opportunity to strike.

"These were the evidence I brought before the King as a loyal subject with a heavy heart," Morcant jeered. "Evidence of atrocities I felt had to be answered for, atrocities against the people of a loving king. Yes, these arrowheads are unique to your young Oskara friends, Rekin and Rylr, are they not? And these bits of pendant when placed together fit the color and shape of your own. Finally, the head to bring the severity of the matter to the forefront. This made the kettle boil over, you might say. All there was left to do, as your father had already replaced you as heir, was to bring about a meeting between you. What else could he do but banish you from not only the country but the royal family as well?"

"What of your scouts, you may be thinking. What indeed." Turning to one of the guards, Morcant nodded. The soldier turned and walked behind the throne, opening a hidden door in the wall. Out tumbled four men, bound and gagged, pushed from behind by a misshapen form holding a short curved sword.

Dread crept through Ethan as he recognized the men he had sent. "What have you done to these men? They are loyal soldiers of your king!"

Morcant glared at him, "Loyal? Loyal to you, yes, but not this throne. They are simply a part of your poison infecting this city. My associate here is adept at rooting out such infection." Fell, as it was he that followed the scouts, cackled and thrust his blade into the back of the neck of the closet man.

"No!" cried Ethan, lunging towards the killer, spear tips breaking his skin as he raged against the surrounding soldiers. It was no use, Fell slowly and methodically brought the sword up and sliced open the necks of the other three scouts before disappearing back through the hidden door.

Slumping in pain and despair, Ethan managed to spit out, "What do you want from me, spineless dog?"

"Me? I only want to support my king in his decision and decree." The smile was gone now, a baleful light gleamed in the dark eyes. "You will leave and never return. A thorn plucked out and cast away. These highly trained guards, I think you had a hand in the training of some, will show you the way to the outskirts of MY HOUSE! I rule this city now."

B LASH TURNED TOWARDS THE sound of breaking wood and saw his young friend stalking through the door. The tavern door lay twisted from Ethan's entrance. Sighing, Blash shrugged at the tavern keeper and tossed a gold coin his way. To Ethan, "You look as if the very gods of thunder battled inside you. What has happened?"

As he slammed himself onto a bench, rattling

the tankards on tables around the room, Ethan bit out, "We must go from this place. It is no longer a place of welcome to us and ours. Banishment has been issued by the King himself."

Taken aback, Blash studied him. "What were the stated reasons behind such a foolish move might I ask?"

"There is too much pain in the telling, my friend. Wait and I will tell you at a later time." Ethan closed his eyes and shook his head. "We have little time ahead. Gather what soldiers are loyal to you and meet me outside the city on the road leading north."

"It will be done, and in good time too. I will tell the brother captains as well." Blash stood and readied himself to leave. "What is the mission?"

Ethan looked him in the eyes, "Protection. Protection of all we love and all we have sworn to serve. We must do what others will not and hunt down these wraiths. We must close the passes from the coastal plains into the greater Astar lands." He sighed and stood with Blash. "I only hope enough will come."

14
THE STEAM YARDS

EARLY IN THE MORNING Oliver and the two goblin brothers made their way to the upper halls of the Deep Fallows. From there they headed West to the steam docks that overlooked the Beryl Sea far below. A large part of the food supply for the city and the outlying villages came from fishing along the coast. Though it was still before dawn, the docks were a frenzy of activity as fishermen and dock workers went about preparations for the day's labor.

The docks stretched out from the surrounding rock wall, platforms hanging precariously from cables over the open air. A number of rail cars rumbled between the platforms and ships, ferrying supplies and workers. Coal fires were being stoked in furnaces at the rear of the docks to heat the massive caldrons of water fit into the walls. The resulting steam was carried by a maze of pipes to all corners of the dockyards, some to the ships themselves.

The ships, Oliver noticed, were unlike the smooth, graceful hulled vessels he was accustomed to. Roughly rectangular in shape the steam ships were barge-like things with massive keels to keep them steady on the rough seas. Gray iron pipes ran along the gunnels and into the main control cabins, squat windowed buildings in the center of the decks. The pipes carried the steam from tanks located at the aft of the ships. These tanks were filled by the dockyard pipe networks and had fires to maintain the steam in its current state throughout the day's use. The hearts of the ships were located inside the control cabins, great steam engines that powered the large double-screw propellers to provide thrust. The navigation was done using a common rudder system. The entire propulsion system hung well below the bottom of the hull.

A crew of ten or so navigated the ships and worked the large nets used to snare the fish and rock crabs that inhabited the base of the cliffs.

Farl led the way into the morning light across the creaking planks of the platforms. Oliver felt light headed as he saw the ocean waters glisten far below. Calling to a nearby goblin who appeared to hold a position of leadership at the docks, Farl motioned to the others to drop the packs and gear they carried.

Moving towards them, the foreman eyed Oliver suspiciously, "What can I do for you gents this fine morning?" Farl replied by handing him a letter from Bosgar and waited for the other to read through it. "I will be a flying can of worms if this don't fit nicely into my daily schedule!" Grinning, the foreman beckoned for the three to follow him. He nimbly moved towards the largest of the moored ships, yelling directions to a loitering group of workers who scrambled to gather up the company's packs and equipment.

On closer inspection the ship looked less and less able to float, though the more pressing issue in Oliver's mind was the distance of several hundred feet separating the docks from the water.

Once the gear was stored in lock boxes along the cabin, Oliver and the two brothers were introduced to the captain and his crew. Wind-worn and hardy looking, the goblins that operated the craft were a jovial bunch. They welcomed the chance to change the repetition of their daily work by transporting the three across the channel. Calling out a farewell, the foreman lumbered back to his duties and left them to stand and watch the preparations going on around them.

It seemed as though the majority of the tasks had already been completed and the ship was ready in minutes. Using a horn to amplify his voice across the dockyards, the captain called, "Hook up tether and seat the rails!" Almost instantly the ship jolted violently, spilling Oliver onto his back and he struggled, red-faced, to get his feet back underneath him. Stifling laughter, his comrades held onto the gunwales and helped him up.

The jolt had been caused by the connection of a large cable and gearbox to the aft and fore decks. Soon after a team of workers came alongside the ship and used a massive pulley system to lift the entire vessel until it hung unattached from the dock. A second, farther group pulled on additional cables that gently swung the ship out from the dock and over a solitary cable of immense thickness. It was all Oliver could do to hold on and watch as the crashing waves echoed from far below. His apprehension was only raised when one of the crew came over to the three and secured them to the gunwale with rope harnesses.

Two of the crew then climbed over the side of the ship and reached down to attach harnesses to the larger cable underneath. Rings of steel were swung shut, enclosing the main cable and then hammered secure. As the crew did this, dock workers connected the cables above to a guide chain.

Once the crew members were on deck once

more, the captain called again, "Seated to rail cables, release tether!"

Oliver's stomach plummeted along with the ship! The instant the tethers were disconnected, the ship dropped onto the massive lower cable with a bang and fell like a stone towards the water beneath. The cables attached to the ship above held the ship upright as it fell. Oliver caught his breath, then struggled to hold on and keep breathing as the rocks below grew closer at a frightening speed. A mere sixty feet above the water the cable and guide chain, to this point having hung straight, began to level out heading into the channel. The cry of, "Brace for impact!" came from the captain and was echoed by the crew. As the bow struck the water the cable system went horizontal and the captain released the connections from the rail cables. The ship rocketed across the water like the stones that Oliver had skipped as a boy.

Seconds later the pounding and bouncing that seemed to threaten to tear the ship apart ceased and they floated in relative calm. Tears streaming down his face from the wind of the fall, Oliver retched over the side.

15
ACROSS THE WATER,
UP THE MOUNTAIN

OLIVER WAS STILL RECOVERING from the controlled plunge to the sea when the steamship captain called to his crew to release the steam. Two crewmen made their way to the aft steam tanks and rotated several levers. A hissing sound filled the air as the steam trapped in the tanks escaped down the tubes towards the engines in the hull of the ship. A low rumble signaled the engines catching and the crewmen once again came over and checked the trio's tie-downs. Gulping past the panic that rose at this sign of further danger, Oliver braced himself.

With a roar the ship jumped forward as the propellers caught and sped up. The deck seemed to rise, and as Oliver looked over the side he saw the water fall away until they were suspended twenty feet above it. Long metal beams he had not seen before had unfolded from the hull and now two narrow hull-like platforms bracketed the ship. He now saw why the propellers had been set at such a deep depth as they now were just a few yards beneath the churning waters. Skrit shouted in his ear, "I have heard of these, but never saw them in use. They are called foils and allow for much faster speeds and the ability to navigate shallow waters!" Oliver simply nodded and continued concentrating on his white-knuckled grip.

It seemed only minutes after their speed had risen that the docks located on the foothills of the Shadowmyst Mountains appeared. Soon enough the vessel slowed, and sank back into the water as its engines were throttled down. Head spinning at the speed of the journey from the Goblin City, Oliver untied his harness and joined the crew at the gangway as the ship smoothly floated the last few yards.

After the tie ropes were thrown and secured, the captain led the way across the gangway and onto the solid dock. "Here you are, me boyos, hope the ship did you good! Aerates the liver, eh?" He chuckled at their faces as the trio rushed to dry land. "We be off as there be fish to catch. Light the signal fire on the coast ahead when you be wanting to return!"

Waving their unspoken thanks, the three sank to the ground as the crew threw their packs onto the dock and readied the ship to reverse course. Seconds later the sounds of the steamship faded into the distance.

Oliver turned to the Goblin brothers, sighed, then took up his pack and began to walk towards the marked trailhead far off down the shore. The trail wound through the foothills and steadily rose until Oliver and his companions had to scramble up on all fours. The climb was grueling and they frequently stopped to catch their breath in the thinning air. During the rests, Oliver looked in awe at the panorama that spread beneath them, the base of the mountains beginning to become indistinct in a foggy haze. The towering peaks around them seemed to throw themselves towards heaven and as he looked around he had the unsettling feeling that the mountains were not quite stable, balancing on tip-toes as they vied for first place. Once the thought had entered his mind he could not shake it. As they continued higher and higher his fear of these giants locked in internal struggle grew until he swore that the mountainside under him swayed. He was so focused on not letting the nausea take hold, that he missed a handhold and began to fall backward, arms failing!

Skrit, just below Oliver, jammed a muscled arm into the hillside and caught the falling seeker with the other. He held tight until Oliver was able to find purchase on the slope.

Shaking, Oliver clung to the rock, trying to bring his breathing under control. Farl cautiously made his way back down from above until the three were huddled together. Taking out a coil of rope he tied one end around his waist and then did the same for Oliver and Skrit.

They continued the climb, with the security of the rope giving Oliver some of the confidence he had lost in the fall. An hour later, during a short rest, it looked as though they had moved no more than a few feet in relation to the surrounding mountains and the grasslands below. Looking up they could not make out any changes in the hillside that would mark their goal. Glancing at each other ruefully, they gulped down a meager meal of hard bread and water and began to climb once more.

Dusk began to fall, shadows chasing each other across the rock in front of them, making it harder to find handholds. The sun seemed to mock their task by falling faster and faster into the west and was soon blocked from view by the peaks ahead.

What made it worse were the clouds that concealed the moon as it rose behind them. In this near darkness they continued to struggle upwards looking for the deeper black of an opening in the rock. After several near falls, Skrit called for a halt. They were discussing how they would tie themselves to the mountainside so that they could rest, when Oliver caught sight of movement above them.

A small mountain goat peered down from a ledge of some kind no more than forty feet away. With a muffled shout of relief, Oliver pointed towards the ledge as the goat, startled by the outburst, disappeared. Heartened once more they climbed to the ledge and discovered a shallow grass-filled outcropping. The goat was nowhere in sight.

Oliver dropped his pack and sat down against it with a sigh, stretching his aching limbs. The brothers followed suit, still connected to each other by the rope. Farl stretched his shoulders and looked around, peering into the darkness of the cliff walls that bordered the ledge. "Well and good that we made it here, but how far back it goes I wonder."

Oliver tried to reply but exhaustion pulled at his body, and his eyelids fell shut as he quickly fell asleep.

Skrit looked at Farl and laughed, "I am for following the boy." He tied the rope to an outcropping and soon the only sounds that could be heard were the snores of tired men.

THE FIRST RAYS OF the morning sun were struggling against the darkness when Oliver woke. As he pushed himself onto his knees and turned towards the cliff edge, the view took his breath away. His senses strained to fathom the scene before him. Far below the ocean waters crashed against the strip of land at the base of the cliffs. Gray and brown rock fell towards the lavender foothills that rose to meet them. Across the narrow channel of water and stretching for miles were the gray-green grasslands of the main island bordered by the dark blue of the lake that surrounded what remained of his home. Wisps of low lying clouds drifted past beneath the ledge. A hawk circled above the faint outline that was the road from the Goblin city to the Astar cities. Oliver thought he could even make out the dim shapes of the masts of ships that lay at anchor in the great Astar shipyards on the far eastern coast. It was all framed by the red gold hue of the morning sun as its light stretched towards him, finally warming him and taking away some of the chill of the mountain night. The sunlight swept down the mountainside, encouraging the morning roses that clung to the rocks to unfold and welcome the life-giving rays. Down and down the light raced as it dissipated the clouds, brightening the landscape until gray was green and brown was gold. It took his breath away.

His known world was laid out like a map, making it seem smaller and larger simultaneously.

His companions slowly joined him and they stood at the edge of their world for many minutes in silence. Eventually hunger forced them to tear their eyes away and dig through their packs for a meager breakfast. Once they were done eating they looked closer at the ledge itself. It was small and it did not take long before they were happily surprised. A narrow path led into the mountainside through a partially hidden cleft in the rock. Small hoof prints marked the stone, revealing the goat's escape route.

Pulling on their packs and checking the straps on their weapons they took a last look at the brightening panorama, and then made their way into the cleft.

16
HELK GORGE

ETHAN STOOD OVERLOOKING THE Helk Gorge and attempted to focus his thoughts on the task at hand. It had been a frantic few days as he cobbled together the troops loyal to him and then traveled to establish a defensive perimeter in the wooded Highlands north of the Foar River. He had chosen this ground as the primary defensive site due to the valley that sloped from his level and fell away into the gorge. The cleft marked the beginning of the lower lands and was the only passage large enough for any significant force onto the plateau, and from there into the greater Highlands. The walls of the gorge jutted straight up then stretched north for a distance, causing the floor of the gorge to resemble a trough. This gave him the ability to stage forces along the ridges and rain death down on any approaching enemy. In times past enemies had invaded from the north, necessitating the continual manning of a small outpost overlooking the gorge. In recent years the outpost had been neglected for posts closer to the coast in the lowlands. There had been no word from those outposts and he presumed them destroyed.

Ethan turned from the gorge's edge and walked back towards the encampment that housed his command of two hundred footmen. The command was broken down into fifty man detachments, each led by an Oskara captain. The Astar soldiers were joined by a small contingent of Seeker Mystics. The small force was all that could be raised before news of Ethan's banishment spread. Close on the heels of Ethan's departure from the castle a proclamation went out that stated all who followed Ethan and his doomed comrades would be deemed deserters. Their families would be taxed each day the soldier was gone and any grown sons would be forced into the Royal Guards. The message, spread far and wide, met with mixed results. Some that had been loyal to Ethan balked and sorrowfully told him that they could not put their families through such a thing. Others eagerly volunteered, their loyalties inflamed out of anger at the government's decree. The soldiers who were now encamped above the gorge had sent their families to the far west, near the hills of the Goblins, to wait for their return.

Blash greeted him with a grunt and slowly eased his massive bulk into a standing position. He looked in the direction Ethan had come from and grinned, displaying gaping holes where teeth had once been. "I feel in my bones that in this adversary we will find a true challenge, and my hammer has grown over with mold. It has been too long since blood has washed its stone."

Ethan clapped him on the arm, "You and I, friend, will have much to glory in soon enough. Call our brothers to the Borg Stone for the final planning." The Borg Stone had been the signpost of entry into Astar lands as far back as the great wars at the dawn of recorded history and was now surrounded by a makeshift headquarters.

As Blash turned and strode towards the watch fires, Ethan quietly spoke to a silhouette standing in the shadow of a nearby krin tree, "Altamaeus, are the machines placed?"

The wiry form detached from the shadows and a young Seeker appeared. He was dressed in the simple white tunic of an academic but his cloak was utilitarian, pockets of all sizes covered the dark brown leather, holding his tools of trade. "I supervised the placement myself, my lord. All is ready."

"Well done, my friend," Ethan said with a weary smile, "come with me to the Stone and tonight our plan will be decided."

The Knights and the Mystic deliberated long into the night. As the first glimmer of sun broke through the night sky, they finally stood and headed to their specific commands to conduct final preparations.

Dawn broke as the final tasks were nearing completion and the undersized army was set in place. Midway down the Helk Gorge, Ethan paced the valley floor where he had strung two of the fifty man detachments in a double line, creating a solid wall blocking all movement up the slope. Imbedded into each detachment were two Seekers, clothed in light mail tunics and wearing the pocketed cloaks of their order. Armed with simple iron tipped staves, the mystics relied on their knowledge of the arcane and various solar-fed creations to support the soldiers in battle. Each one had their many pockets filled with non-conventional weapons, ranging from Sun Fire Orbs, which when broken could turn night into day or blind oncoming enemies, to Solar Dust that could burn through armor and flesh. These Seekers also had the ability to project small fields of power around friendly soldiers that would absorb the impact of enemy attacks for a limited time.

The remaining detachments under Blash's command were divided and placed along the top of the gorge walls. Their task was to provide covering fire with crossbows and to protect the remaining Seekers and the hulking contraptions they were working on. They were also prepared to act as a quick reaction force to come to the aid of the soldiers in the gorge as needed.

As the Seekers on the bluffs pulled leather covers off the great machines the cliff heights exploded in light. The light faded quickly as it was drawn into the giant devices themselves.

Evidence of years of research, the machines were the pride of Altamaeus and his Seeker followers. Standing upwards of twelve meters tall, formed of polished metals and framed by great wooden beams, two of the machines stood at either side of the gorge on the cliff top and on each, three great metal wings stretched skyward. The wings were made of an iron composite covered in thin layers of yellow quartz to catch the sun's rays and draw the light down into the body of the machine where mirrored tubes condensed and funneled the solar energy into a lead shielded box that stored the converted energy. A lever opened a small door at the far end of the box allowing a stream of light out through a set of rose quartz that intensified it into a powerful beam of energy capable of burning anything in its path. Though dependent on sunlight, the machines could store a limited amount of energy for use at night or when clouds hid the sun. Already the growing daylight was surging through the machines and building up the required energy.

It was midday before the waiting Astar and Seekers heard the approaching enemy. The surrounding brushland went deathly quiet; and a low drumming began to echo off the gorge walls. Slowly the Northern horizon faded from blue, open sky to a gray haze as the smoke of countless torches trailed the approaching enemy. The drumming grew louder and the well-known beat of armored boots shook the ground. A sentry perched on the cliffs sounded his horn, marking the enemy's arrival into view as Ethan turned to his footmen.

"This day, this day we will make history in bloodshed!" His cry echoed along the gorge and was answered by the booming crash of two hundred swords on shields. Ethan clasped arms with Captains Rekin and Rylr and turned to face the oncoming enemy.

A sense of calm settled over him as he caught

sight of the forerunners of the enemy force. The first shape that crashed through the surrounding forest and stopped in the open was black as night. A two legged thing, the creature stood near seven feet tall and was covered in glistening dark armor from boots to helm. A long jagged saber hung at its side, and a great double bladed axe was grasped in a taloned fist.

The long, narrow face swung in Ethan's direction and a gleam of fire glittered within its deep-set eyes as it uttered a command in a strange rasping tongue to unseen followers. The surrounding forest exploded as nearly two score of the dark creatures crashed into the open and followed the first in a mad rush towards the waiting Astar footmen.

17
SHADOWLANDS

THE PATH WAS JUST large enough to allow their passage. At first level, the trail began to rise and the leaves from overhanging branches could be seen above them. They walked for hours before the sun marked noonday and the path leveled out once more and widened until they could walk side by side.

Grass and flowers began to appear, the trunks of trees came into view and they heard the sounds of birds and other animals. When they came upon on a small stream flowing with crystal clear water they stopped to eat and rest their weary backs. They were on the edge of a small glade, the way they had come clearly different from what lay ahead. Behind them were rock walls and small scrub trees stretching towards the sunlight. Ahead was a wall of the largest trees any of them had ever seen, the trunks wider than the length of a large horse and covered in a silvery gray bark that shone in the darkness under the boughs that towered above. Shadows danced within the mist that floated just above the moss covered ground. Sunlight struggled to break through the dense canopy, shafts of gold stabbed down towards the forest floor and illuminated the way ahead in hazy, disconnected islands of light.

Knowing that dusk was not far off, Farl recommended that they pitch camp along the stream and venture into the wood the next day. Oliver, looking into the darkness creeping through the forest, could not find any reason to disagree.

They spread out their gear and Skrit and Oliver gathered wood while Farl prepared a fire pit with smooth stones from the creek. Once the fire had started and a stew of vegetables and fish was warming, Oliver asked, "Ever since we left your underground city, I have thought of the impossibility of its existence."

Laughing, Farl slapped him on the back, "There be secrets below, young sir! While the world watched the Goblins flourish and expand from a small town to a city and outlying villages, we dug. Deep into the earth we went, a hundred years our people labored against the rock. We mined and used the ores that entwined through the hills and became experts at the molding of it. The steel we wrought into all manner of things brought the name of Steelforge to the surface city. The outside world knew that the metals in their wares had to have come from somewhere, but no one had seen the source. Until forty years ago."

Oliver was surprised at this, "Why did you keep it a secret and what happened back then?"

"The second question will I answer first," chortled Farl. "A man chased by war found the entrance. He hid himself there, not knowing how far the cave went until those who pursued him had left. There in sleep did our father, not yet a leader, find him and bring him down, deep into the hills. To the wall at the entrance to the throne room he brought him. The excavation had not begun past the gate at that time." A shadow fell over Farl's face, "His act was looked upon as a betrayal of our nation's greatest secret. Our underground spaces, burrowed out in preparation of a time men or their like would tire of us. Now our father brought one of those men inside. Blood was spilled that night as our father stood over the unconscious body of the stranger and fought off those who would have slain him to keep our secret."

Farl paused to ladle stew out of the boiling pot and Skrit took over the tale, "The goblin leader at the time learned of this and came to be witness to it. He bade the attackers fall back and questioned our father for many hours. The agreement that was forged between them is how we relate to others to this day. If there is a dire need that we Goblins have the power to fill, it is our duty to life to do so. Our father changed the dynamic that existed before that time. No longer were we a fearful people overshadowed by dire futures. We became a strong nation that supports the weak among us all."

Nodding in agreement, Farl continued, "The man woke soon after and was nearly out of his mind trying to figure out where he was. Once the goblin leader and our father explained what had happened the man knelt and offered his life in service as repayment. Goblins had never before been afforded such respect from a tall one and our leader assured the man that no debt existed. The man stayed for days, learning more of our people. When he began preparations to leave, he spoke to our father. He laid a burden on him, apologizing all the while. He was to look after the one that would come seeking help in time of need. One who would need guidance and passage to the Shadowmyst Mountains."

As he poured stew for Oliver, Skrit whispered, "You are that one, young friend."

EARLY THE NEXT DAY, Oliver made his way along a narrow path through the dense forest as the early morning light attempted to weave its way through the canopy. He had left his companions at the campsite to think through the story they had told him the night before. He marveled at the enormity of it all. How could he be a part of something so large, stretching over decades? He keenly felt his lack of experience. Wandering without thought to direction, his feet sent him down a gentle slope through the wood.

Suddenly noticing the warmth of the sun on his face, he found himself at the edge of the wood and looked out across a small valley. He stood in astonishment at the beautiful sight. Wrapped by a close circle of forest lay a mountain-fed lake glistening in the morning sun, gentle waterfalls thundered in the distance, and drinking in the silver shallows were dozens of strange creatures the size of ponies. They were unlike anything he had ever seen, long bodies standing on six crooked legs that ended in handlike claws. Their heads were long and narrow, a strange mixture of birds' eyes and wolf muzzle, with long tongues lapping at the water. Golden birds the size of half-grown children were gliding in lazy circles above the water, dipping into the water time and again to draw out wriggling creatures to feast on. The slopes of the valley were covered with flowers that exploded with intense color as they drank up the sun's morning light and became their own brightly colored stars.

Before he had time to even begin to grasp the wonder of the panorama before him, a sound like a gentle breeze sighed past him, inexplicably causing a feeling somewhere between apprehension and terror, rooting him to the ground. Something softly touched his shoulder and drawing his dagger, he spun around, breath caught in his throat. There was nothing in sight, just the empty path he had followed and the calm of the shaded wood. Nervously chiding himself, he turned back to the lake and immediately threw himself back in fright! Not two feet away stood a tall thin figure wrapped in a dark cloak.

The thing was hooded and had the rising sun at its back, making it seem only a shadow. He vainly attempted to gain control over his limbs, but collapsed onto the ground, and stared up at the apparition from a seated position. He regained enough control to remove his hand from his dagger, making a desperate gesture of peace. A sighing whisper of a voice, edged in steel, emanated from the darkness of the hood, "What are you to appear alone and unarmed?" As it spoke the figure turned its head and fixed a glowing eye on Oliver. The eye more than the voice shocked him as he involuntarily gaped at the deep green eye with catlike pupil ringed with flecks of gold.

He struggled to articulate words, "I...I mean, that is I am...I was," a queer thought suddenly sprang to mind and he blurted, "sent by Magnus".

With a feline scream the figure lunged towards him and before he could move, held two wicked crescent shaped blades to his throat. "Tell me where you heard this name! " was hissed through pointed teeth as the strange face drew close.

Unleashing his fear with a surge of blue fire, Oliver threw the figure off and hurled it several yards away as he struggled to his feet. With feline grace the figure landed on its feet and leapt past him only to spring off a tree and come for his head from behind, blades flashing with inhuman quickness.

Oliver threw his right arm up in a protective stance and surrounded himself with a shield of golden light just as his adversary reached him. One blade had come too close to be completely blocked and became trapped in the haze of light, snapping in two as the dark figure fell back to the ground.

Surprisingly, the creature calmly stood and

studied him, hood thrown back to reveal dark green hair that surrounded a pale narrow face void of expression. Its features were vaguely human except for the eyes and four fang-like teeth protruding from the top and bottom of its mouth.

Fearing the stranger was thinking of new ways to attack, Oliver breathlessly choked out an answer to the previous question; "My teacher and friend, Magnus himself set me on the path that led to this place. Magnus of the Sun Fire Citadel."

As he uttered the Citadel's name, the figure spun, leapt, and vanished into the trees without a sound. For a split second, Oliver thought he had seen a flash of fear on the creature's face.

18
DAY OF FIRE

THE LEADER OF THE beasts raced towards the footmen who were braced for impact. It saw Ethan
raise his great sword in signal and it instinctively
reached behind and swung one of its followers to
take its place. The rushing wind of crossbow bolts
whirled past the leader's head and crashed into
the front ranks of the dark command, causing the
first line of creatures to smash to the ground in a
convulsing mass. Dropping the now limp body,
the leader beast leapt forward and swung its great
axe at the nearest footman, slicing through shield
and armor, killing him instantly. Continuing its
momentum, it leapt forward with a hissing bellow and swung the great axe at Ethan who caught
the blow on his sword and twisted, attempting to
spin his enemy to the ground. Rather than falling,
the black thing spun with inhuman agility into the
first rank of footmen, axe whirling. Cries of pain

and the sickening thud of bodies connecting with sharp metal echoed as the remaining enemy joined in the fray with sabers flashing.

Losing sight of the enemy leader, Ethan found himself surrounded by three of the hulking beasts. Lowering a shoulder he bowled one over as he slashed at another, feeling his blade bite deep into the creature. Hissing in pain it stumbled back and fell clutching at its ruined leg just as a crossbow bolt to the neck ended its life. Ethan spun around to see the last creature's saber arcing towards his neck. He threw himself back, and the enemy's saber burst in a shower of molten sparks as a Seeker's Solar Dust disintegrated the metal, leaving the beast swinging the now worthless hilt. As the creature paused in surprise, a footman drove his sword into its side, crippling the thing as Ethan swung the killing blow.

The battle was quick and fierce; the enemy leader's rush into the Astar defensive line had instantly killed two footmen and wounded three others before Rekin came to their aid with a bellow, broadsword crashing against axe as he fought to bring the great creature down. His blow drove the enemy's axe into the ground but as Rekin drew back his sword to exploit the opening, the beast dropped its axe and charged into him, armored fists hammering at his helm. Dazed, he stumbled back and brought his sword forward in an attempt to stop his adversary's advance. Too late Rekin saw a flash of metal as the creature drove a long knife towards his weak underarm armor. Instead of slicing through in a fatal blow, the blade shattered against a pulsing shield of light cast around him by a nearby Seeker. Kicking out, Rekin fought to regain control of the fight, but the creature spun, recovered its axe and disappeared in the surrounding chaos.

Upon the heights, blash paced impatiently as he watched the melee unfold and called out targets for his crossbowmen. The initial barrage of bolts had not been as effective as he would have liked. The unknown black armor worn by the enemy seemed capable of even turning crossbow bolts at times. Also, a few of the creatures dropped by the bolts had rejoined the battle with seemingly no ill effect. Blash wondered at the source of such a metal and the things that wore it and his fist closed tightly over his war hammer as he fantasized testing how much the enemy armor could truly take before it failed. Behind him the Seekers stood poised next to their machine ready for his signal to put it into operation.

The defensive line below had dissolved into pockets of four or more footmen fighting two or three of the beasts at a time. The things seemed to shrug off wounds that would fell a man. The supporting Seekers darted through the chaos scattering solar dust over the enemy, instantly melting their armor, laying them open to more damage, and blocking killing blows against the footmen with shields of solar energy. Ethan and his captains formed footmen around them and focused their attacks against the creatures with weakened armor, blades slicing through the unprotected white-gray flesh. The battle began to lean towards the defenders favor as they cut the enemy down one by one.

Through the fray Ethan caught sight of the enemy leader and lunged towards the beast. But as Ethan closed in, a harsh cry rang out in the distance and the surviving creatures immediately disengaged from the battle and fled in full retreat back the way they had come, chased by crossbow bolts. The last one to enter the darkness of the woods was the leader; it faced towards the Astar defenders and raised its axe above his head in a flaunting gesture of disdain before it turned and walked out of sight.

Quickly rallying his remaining troops back into

an ordered line, Ethan signaled to Blash to send a small contingent of footmen to carry off the dead and wounded. Running along the line he counted the remaining able men and came to eighty-six of the original hundred. A Seeker ran up and relayed that there were nine dead creatures and that the few wounded enemies had fired an unknown substance into themselves from small burst weapons concealed within the black scale armor. Even as Ethan bent over one of the bodies it began to move, seeming to draw into itself, shrinking until all that remained was the shell of armor. Reaching out to touch the black metal, he quickly drew back his hand as a tendril of smoke started rising from it. They watched in astonishment as, seconds later, all that remained of the creatures' bodies were patches of smoking earth.

R EALIZING THAT THE ENEMY could return in greater numbers at any instant, Ethan called his captains to him, "We have tested these beasts and know they die! The next time they come in numbers; we execute the next step of the plan."

Nodding in agreement, Rekin and Rylr returned to their men to spread the word as Ethan raised a fist to Blash on the bluff heights. Grinning, the bear of a man spoke to the Seeker who was dwarfed beside him. A frenzy of activity erupted around the Seeker's machines as final calibrations were completed and focus sights were aimed.

AT MIDDAY THE CREATURES returned in force and with more caution, treading rank by rank onto the floor of the gorge until it seemed they were an extension of the dark forest.

As Ethan and his force stood at the ready, the same enemy leader pushed to the forefront of the dark command and spoke in hissing Astari; "Good that you stayed, little ones. Our appetites have been whetted."

Ethan, raising a hand to quell Blash's imminent rebuke from above, simply stood and laughed at the creature in answer.

With a roar of rage the beast waved his ranks forward. Shaking the ground, line by line the hulking fighters strode towards the Astar. They had learned from the earlier skirmish and were now outfitted with massive shields to protect them from the archers on the heights.

When twenty yards separated the two forces, Ethan raised a hand. The light of double suns burst from the Seeker's machines on the heights above, causing the enemy to halt in confusion. He dropped his hand and focused beams of light sliced into the creatures, instantly burning through shield, armor, and flesh. It was a slaughter; the entire enemy force that had left the safety of the trees was soon dead or dying. The stench of burning flesh and ozone filled the air as the Seekers continued to sweep the battleground with the solar fed beams, even burning through sections of the forest in search of any remaining enemy.

In minutes the enemy force was a mass of smoldering flesh and smoking armor.

19
THE ASH

OLIVER TRIED TO CATCH his breath as he ran back to the campsite. He found the brothers readying their gear and stomping out the embers that remained in the fire pit. Noticing his rumpled clothes and white face they rushed to his side.

"What has happened, friend?", queried Skrit as he helped Oliver to a seat. Farl offered him a wineskin, "You look as if you saw a ghost of the fey itself!"

Oliver gulped the fiery liquid too quickly and choked and sputtered before being able to answer. "I have a better understanding of the name of these mountains." He went on to tell the goblins what had transpired in the woods. The brothers listened with grave faces.

When Oliver finished, Farl sank to a knee. "Forgive us for allowing this danger to befall you. We were given you as our charge and have come close to failing in this."

"Think not of it again, my friend," admonished Oliver. "I know I will not. What is important is the fact that the name I spoke was recognized. This may be why I was told to come here. I cannot turn away from even the slightest possibility of guidance."

Skrit began to speak then froze in place and held a finger to his lips for silence. The others stilled and waited for him to tell them what was going on. Skrit slowly moved his finger until it pointed towards the trees that bordered the far side of the stream. Oliver did not see anything at first, the sunlight making it hard to see past the shadows of the leaves. Farl started next to him as he caught sight of whatever it was.

Then Oliver saw it. High in a tree stood the feline creature that he had encountered earlier. It leaned against the trunk of the tree in a relaxed pose gazing out at the three of them.

Oliver whispered. "That is the one that I told you of." The brothers nodded and reached for the broad axes at their belts. A short musical laugh stopped them.

"Need you not the weapons, small ones," the creature spoke as it jumped gracefully to the ground and walked to the water. "I am friend to you, though the young one has reason to not trust me." Nodding to Oliver it touched two fingers to its forehead in an elegant sign of respect.

Farl growled, "You may be friend but our weapons will be in hand. What friend attacks another?"

Showing long fangs as it smiled the creature replied, "As warden of these woods, I have need to act when change threatens. Very few venture here and I had to know our world was safe." Crouching to run its hands through the water it spoke again, "Little time remains to us. You are to come with me to my village at the heart of the forest where your questions may be asked of a greater one than I."

Oliver gathered his composure, "What are you, may I ask?"

The creature stood proudly, "I am Ash, as out of the ashes of a failed civilization we came. Now come with me quickly."

The three looked at each other. "If we can find out anything of what I am to do, we must follow," stated Oliver with a look of determination. The goblins nodded in agreement and they all quickly finished breaking down the camp site. Minutes later the three comrades found themselves trotting through the woods in an effort to keep up with their nimble guide. They passed within sight of the meadow Oliver had marveled at earlier, skirting the open land in a sweeping circle before plunging deep into the wood on the far side.

A few hours later they arrived at their destination. The village was located far above the ground, intertwined within the towering trees, rope and plank bridges providing conveyance between the structures. There was no sign of life or any kind of movement. As Oliver and his companions stood and drank in the view, their guide continued forward to an open glade at the center of the grove of trees. Reaching the edge, he put his hands to his lips and blew, emitting a low guttural tone that rang through the trees. An answer came faintly from high above and their guide motioned them to approach and stand beside him. Moving to his side, Oliver thought he began to notice small furtive movements in his periphery. When he turned to catch hold of the source of the motions there was nothing to see. Remembering how his first interaction with the Ash had gone, he was not surprised that the residents of the village remained hidden. Oliver's skin crawled as he attempted to anticipate when they would be confronted by the ones their guide had called to.

His attempts fell far short of being effective and he jumped, nearly tripping over Skrit as a creature materialized inches from his face. Whatever it was, it was the most perplexing creature Oliver had ever seen. It was roughly two feet tall and what made it able to appear at face level was the startling fact that it hovered. Blue fire was his first thought, blue fire encased in a humanoid form with eyes of iridescent green that blazed with cold heat. His voice lost, he stared open mouthed for what seemed forever until the creature spoke. Not in the traditional sense as the creature's lips did not move and yet a tinkling voice danced through their hearing. Ethereal and faint the creature said, "Welcome to Shadowmyst. I am Aethel the forest guide and leader of the Ash and last of the Dauru from across the Beryl Sea. You have been given the gift of entering into our midst, a rare feat and only because of the name you have stated to Feiyr"

Oliver stumbled through a reply, "Thank you for your kindness, I am Oliver of the Sun Fire Citadel, and these are my companions, brothers Farl and Skrit." We have come to the Shadowmyst Mountains on a quest that was placed in my hands uninvited."

The fire creature asked, "How do you come to be here and why has Magnus sent you in his stead?"

Oliver started in surprise, "How do you know

of my friend and teacher?"

"It was he, the first human in this place, who began the sequence that now brings you here," Aethel trilled. "It was many rotations of the sun ago when he came to me, speaking of a dark insidious evil that was only just becoming more than thought in the lands. He had come to ask my guidance on who might be the one who would bring the darkness to pass, but at the time my sight was unable to pull away the veil that hid the truth."

Farl stepped forward suddenly. "One of light, I am Farl of the Deep Fallows. This man you speak of, did he come near to forty rotations ago?"

Cold realization flooded through Oliver at the creature's reply, "Well met, rock dweller. I have watched with great interest the change that came over your people shortly after the man I spoke of left us. Forty years would be correct."

Skrit turned to Oliver excitedly, "Your mentor was the one we spoke of. The one our father fought for!" Oliver felt like he had been hit in the gut as the realization washed over him. He thought he had known and understood Magnus but he had never spoken of his travels or his interaction with the Goblins or others. He felt betrayed in some way. Why had his friend and teacher held all this from him?

Looking up, Oliver noticed that the Dauru was watching him intently. "I see that this man is connected deeply to those of this world, but that he kept it a closely guarded secret." Aethel moved closer, "Dwell not on the gaps in your knowledge of his life. You are part of his legacy now, he lives on through you."

Oliver asked, "Can you tell me more of this quest that I have found myself on? All I know of it is that I was to follow the directions that led me to these mountains. For what purpose?" Oliver's voice rose, threatening to break, "All those I knew and loved are dead, and alone I have pursued something I have no grasp of!"

A breath of cool air swept over his face and he stopped as a fiery hand touched his face. "Please follow me. We will sit and rest as we speak," Aethel whispered. "What I have learned since Magnus came to us is little, but it may go a long way to providing guidance for your task."

Feiyr led the way to an open bluff at the edge of the village and produced three small wooden stools, he himself remained standing, feral eyes in ceaseless movement. The sun began to fall into the western peaks, the moon rising before them as they sat. Dusk swallowed them quickly.

20
MIDNIGHT WATCH

AFTER VIEWING THE CARNAGE created by the Seeker's weapons, Ethan and his soldiers stood in shock as silence pervaded the gorge. Minutes went by until Blash came down off the heights and stopped beside his commander. Wordlessly they looked at each other, a grim smile on Blash's face.

"It seems to be something less than right the way they fell, as if the very heavens struck them down. My hands ache from not striking them myself and my mind cannot fathom the slaughter."

Serious, Ethan replied; "I have no sorrow for the beasts but the speed of this destruction has affected me as well." They stood for several more minutes looking at the littered ground before Ethan left the older man to call the captains together and set about establishing a stronger defensive position. The look on Blash's face worried Ethan as he walked away, the big man was not one to show uncertainty.

An hour had gone by before Ethan made the decision to send scouts into the tree line. A squad of five footmen slowly moved into the darkness of the woods and were quickly lost from sight.

Instead of the explosion of noise and the cries of battle that he expected, Ethan was surprised when the scouting party returned within the hour and came to him to report. "Sir, we went as far as a quarter mile into the woods until we came out the other side and then followed the edge of the forest for another quarter mile to either side. Though we saw the results of the passage of many creatures on the terrain, we saw neither the main body or scouts of the enemy force."

Confused but relieved, Ethan went to relay the information to Blash. The big man was pacing on the heights and Ethan was greeted with a questioning look. "Friend, tell me of this Altameaus and how you came to meet such a frightening creature. I must know more of the power he wields to be comfortable with him nearby. Having witnessed such slaughter, I cannot reconcile him in my mind."

Nodding in understanding Ethan replied, "Forgive me for keeping you in the dark, it was not my purpose. The events of late kept my mind tied up. We met as boys when I was sent away from the palace, most likely to rid my family the trouble of my presence." He smiled grimly. "It was at the Sun Fire Citadel that we were brought together as schoolmates in training on the powers latent in the sun. We were kindred spirits, he wishing to journey far and wide, and I having done so. I related my knowledge and he schooled me in his." He paused suddenly.

Blash took a seat on a nearby boulder and nodded his encouragement for Ethan to continue.

"It was a dark morning a year after I had arrived at the Sun Fire Citadel. We had taken a small boat and gone to the lake's shore to hunt the large lizards that roamed the reeds. An older Seeker broke through the trees and ran towards us shouting for us to sail away. He was harried by a score or more of what looked to be well-equipped bandits. I being the stubborn lad you well know, did no such thing," Ethan winked. "With only a bow and staff did we come to the man's aid. Altameaus saved me that day. With a contraption he had hidden even from me, he held the men off until the three of us managed to wound or kill enough to dissuade the others from continuing the attack. The machine was eventually turned into what the Seekers now use to conjure shields. The Seeker was weak with fatigue and loss of blood and we ferried him to the island and brought him to the healers. Little did we know at the time, but he was one of the highest of the Seekers just returned from a decade long journey of some great significance. What, we never learned. His name was Manus or Magnus I think. No matter, I was shortly after taken into the Oskara school in Aster Terrace where you and I first met." Ethan sank to the ground, tired to his bones.

"I did not hear from Altameaus for years. Then the well-known rumors began of a renegade Seeker breaking away from the order at the Citadel. I instinctively knew it was my friend. Over the years I have tried to keep track of him and found that he led a secretive group of Seeker mystics named the 'Black Watch' known to experiment on and produce the most powerful war machines in the known world."

Blash shook his head and chuckled, "The people that are drawn to you are a motley bunch!" Ethan grinned wryly and nodded. The two men sat in silence for long minutes until Altameaus walked up. Ethan welcomed the Seeker and laid out his plans, "We will hold position here and send sentries past the woods to give us early warning of an approaching attack."

As the sun began to sink, the main force was divided into two groups that would take turns keeping watch and getting much needed food and rest on the heights.

D ARKNESS FELL, ETHAN, STANDING next to one of the machines on the bluff sensed an unnatural shade of color to the clouds that rolled across the sky, obscuring the moon, causing him to wonder if some magics were in play. He shivered in the chill night breeze and thought through the day's events.

They had been fortunate, the mass of enemy forces had sounded as if they could have swept the defenders aside like dead leaves, yet it seemed the enemy was content to be cautious and feel out the threat. The solar weapons had evidently had a demoralizing effect.

As he thought Ethan walked through the small medical tents placed nearby and spoke to the several wounded soldiers, offering a hand of encouragement and a kind word. The Seeker in charge of the medical staff walked with him and gave him details on each of the soldiers' conditions. A few would most likely not see daylight, and these he spent more time with, accepting messages to loved ones and assuring them of their bravery during the fighting.

Trembling with exhaustion, Ethan finally sat at the base of the nearest machine and was slowly giving up in his fight to stay awake when an explosion of fire and piercing light erupted from the direction of the Seeker machine on the far side of the gorge entrance.

Suddenly wide awake, he leapt to his feet and hurled himself towards the sound. As he moved he called out to the footmen laying around him and he was soon joined by a score of men. Flames ignited ahead, silhouetting the solar machine as torches were thrown against it by dark shapes. In the glare several footmen and Seekers could be seen locked in combat with the attackers, blue fire striking out at the enemy.

Ethan swept through the madness and sliced at the nearest foe, his blade taking its head from its shoulders. These creatures were smaller than the ones they had fought the day before. Short and sinewy, the things were covered in slimy green-brown skin. Their weapons were braces of long knives that they used with great proficiency, blocking strikes and cutting at the unprotected faces and limbs of the humans.

Ethan and the reinforcements were quickly cutting the enemy down when the ground shook and a mammoth creature stalked out of the darkness followed by more of the smaller ones. The giant carried a jagged mace of iron and stone and was covered in broad scales that made the creature seem hewn from stone.

At the same time Blash's horn sounded and he, Altameaus, and several other men joined the fight from the rear of the lumbering beast. Blash's war cry was covered by the sounds of his hammer clashing against the armored monster. Altameaus spun through the smaller creatures, stave whirling, lines of blue flame running its length. Its impact sent the enemy flying, smoking as they tumbled away into the darkness.

Ethan suddenly found himself before the giant creature and barely had time to throw himself to the side as it's mace thudded into the ground beside him. Rolling, he fought to his feet and turned to face the reptilian monstrosity.

The thing wrenched its mace from the ground and fluidly turned towards Ethan, a toothy grin stretching its black skin. Its size belied its grace, its movements were easy and quick and eyes constantly roved, taking in the battlefield. It swung the mace to rest on its shoulder and took a step towards him. It suddenly jerked in surprise as iron bolts sprouted from its side.

Captain Rekin stood fifty feet away with a line

of crossbowmen, directing their fire into the attackers. Within seconds the towering creature stood alone. Blash, finding himself free of other opponents, charged towards the giant's back, swinging his hammer in wide arcs to gain momentum. The creature noticed the charging man and lashed out with its spiked tail. His old joints restricting quick movements, Blash had no choice but to brace for the impact. In mid-swing the tail suddenly burst into crimson flame, withered, and fell away!

Screaming in pain and anger, the creature swung towards the robed figure of Altameaus standing mere feet away and funneling a stream of red flame from a ruby stone held in his fist. The distraction gave Blash the seconds needed to swing his great hammer into the thing's back, scales snapping, bone crunching and giving way. Another wave of bolts embedded themselves into the creatures upper torso, sparks flying from the impact.

Falling under the impact of the weapons, the creature launched itself sideways and onto Altameaus. The Seeker had just enough time to throw up a protective shield before the massive weight of the creature crashed down on him. The shield's light held for a moment, flared, and went out. Rolling away, the giant lurched to its feet again, leaving the body of Altameaus in the crater its impact had created.

Screaming in rage, Ethan threw himself at the creature, swinging his sword two-handed again and again until the blade shattered against its armored hide. Throwing the shards aside, Ethan drew his long knives and kept at the frenzied attack, steadily pounding until gaps and cracks allowed the blades to brings gushes of blood. Unable to shake the frenzied human, the creature beat at him with clawed hands, blows becoming weaker and weaker until its body sagged and it sank to its knees.

Blash pulled Ethan off of the creature and aimed a heavy blow at its head, landing it with a wet crunch. The giant's clawed hands scrabbled at the torn earth and then went still.

Blood, his and the beast's, soaked Ethan's tunic and dented armor. Gasping for breath with tears running down his grime covered face he dropped his weapons and crawled to where Altameaus lay.

Altameaus had been crushed into the ground, but when Ethan bent close he noticed that a shimmering light encased the body of his friend. Startled, he saw that though Altameaus had been pressed into the ground, he was not misshapen, as though his bones had survived the massive weight. The shield must have sustained at least some of its protective quality. As Ethan looked, a low moan emanated from Altameaus and his eyes flickered open.

21
DISCOVERY

SHORTLY BEFORE ETHAN HAD slain the giant creature, Oliver and his companions sat looking out at the mainland to the East and far below. Oliver felt the loneliness of a home far off creep over him as he gazed at the dark mass that held what had once been his. Shaking himself, he tried to concentrate on his host as Aethel began to speak.

"When he first came, Magnus spoke of a darkness." The velvet voice soothed Oliver, and brought him back to the present, "He had been handed down from years past a series of documents that spoke of a threat, an evil rooted in an alchemy of long ago. He entreated me to do what I could to ferret out the source. Over the course of many days the two of us worked, sleep unneeded. Eventually the depth of my knowledge of this world and the world my predecessors had come from was depleted. We had only discovered a few things of significance due to the infancy of the evil."

Aethel paused and drifted closer to the bluff edge and turned to look out at the starry darkness. As the fire being turned back towards the others a flash of soundless brilliance exploded far to the Northeast. The intensity of it grew until without warning it was gone. Blinded, Oliver and the others blinked away the spots that hovered in their vision. "What was that?" asked Farl, squinting in pain.

Feiyr, having ascended the tree he had been leaning against, made the first reply, "It came from the North of your mainland, where the coast meets the high ground. It seemed to me, that torches flared in the same place moments before."

Seeing Oliver's and the goblins' amazed faces, the Dauru said, "Of all Ash, Feiyr has the keenest eyes. This was taken into consideration when the position of warden came to be discussed. A feeling I have of pain and conflict, likely tied to the flash of light we have just seen. I had not heard of war on the mainland of late. Now as we cannot affect what is leagues from us, I shall continue in my tale."

The others took the seats they had jumped from and tried to put the explosion in the back of their minds. Oliver had a sudden hopeful feeling that the flash may have stemmed from the power of another seeker. Maybe he was not alone.

Aethel took up the story again, "What we had discovered was this; an evil the likes of which we had not seen in this world was growing. A seed of darkness had been planted in the heart of someone or something, but we could not discover the exact one. Second, I found long forgotten celestial maps that had been brought to this world by others like me, though their importance was then unclear. Thirdly, and most important to our quest was the knowledge that Magnus would not be the one to eradicate the evil. This was hard to accept, by him most of all, but by me as well. We fought to discover more over the remaining days of that cold autumn. In the end, we came away empty handed, our spirits exhausted."

Aethel came close to Oliver, locking fiery eyes to his, "But we had forgotten in our need to negate what we had learned. In the midst of the knowledge we had studied a boy was spoken of, so young we thought nothing of it in our need for information. This boy would be able to affect this world. Now I see the truth that you, Oliver, be that boy."

Oliver felt his head would explode and he

looked imploringly at his comrades. They only stared back at him.

Aethel continued, "When you came, understanding filled my consciousness. The pieces fit more so than before if still not perfectly. I understand what must be done. I will leave you for a short time to discuss with Feiyr. Rest your minds. I will have refreshment brought to you." The glowing being moved off into the surrounding trees, the tall Ash at its side.

The three companions sat in silence, each one not willing to speak first. Oliver allowed the cool breeze that flowed from the sea far below to relax his mind. His thoughts were a jumble of disconnected facts and he felt he would need days if not longer to work through the experiences of the last few days. Let that work be for tomorrow, he told himself and he closed his eyes.

He woke with a start to find himself face to face with a small female Ash. Arms flailing, he fell off the stool and thudded to the ground amidst laughter from Farl and Skrit. A quiet purring laugh came from the Ash as she reached out to help him to his feet. Red-faced, Oliver brushed off his clothes and sent a dark look towards the goblins.

The Ash couldn't have been full grown, feathery algae blue hair framed the feline features that were freckled with green patches. A smile broke out on the Ash's face and her fangs glistened in the torch light. "Food, I bring," she hissed in a tone that belied her lack of use of his language. She handed Oliver a small basket, like the ones that the goblin brothers were already pulling an assortment of unfamilar nuts and berries from.

Thanking the Ash girl, Oliver accepted the basket and sat down to eat. Once he began eating he realized just how hungry he was. Consumed, he did not notice the Ash whisk away.

The food buoyed the spirits of the three travelers and the goblin brothers began to tell tall tales handed down from generation to generation. Soon their laughter rang against the surrounding forest and out into the open sky.

A small cough broke through their frivolity and they all looked to see Aethel and Feiyr returning. The Ash warden's face was pulled into a snarl, eyebrows pulled together in anger. They could see no change in the Dauru, if a change was even possible and they stood to show respect to their mysterious host.

Feiyr stopped a dozen paces away and glowered at them while Aethel came to hover in their midst. "We have come to an agreement. Though neither is truly at peace with it, it is what must be done. Oliver, come with me." The fiery creature led him along the cliff edge until they were just out of earshot of the others.

"Child," Aethel began, "You have experienced much pain so early. Yet you have come, at times alone. This shows a strength that cannot be taught by words or instruction. Only by experience, yet those who experience the same thing are affected differently. The person they had been, their morals, their senses and preconceived notions color the outcome. Most do not come out the other side of experiences like yours capable of more than keeping themselves alive. Some even cannot bring themselves to do that much and give in to the draw of peace that death tempts them with."

"I tell you this to encourage. There lies a strength inside you that you have not begun to understand. I am putting my trust in this strength. Never be too afraid to believe that you are able to overcome any obstacle you find yourself before."

Listening to these words, Oliver began to worry that his journey had only just begun.

Aethel continued, "Time is at an end. You must listen and try to understand my next words." Oliver bent closer. "When you entered my wood, I had a vision. It was of the time spent with Magnus. The times I had overlooked, that spoke of a boy that would come. More than that though, I finally was given understanding of the use of the star maps I had found." A fiery arm lifted towards the starry sky. "They are a map to be used to hunt down the evil that stirs in this world."

Oliver broke in and asked, "Can I see these maps?" Aethel turned to look at him, the flame's color darkening. "I am afraid they reside only inside me, young one. I will show them to you but first a word. You will meet hardship, lean on your friends." With that statement the being reached out to Oliver. "Place your glove on my hand."

Wondering what the cryptic statement had been about, Oliver did so.

"Now turn on the flow of moonlight," ordered Aethel. As he hit the button with his thumb, Oliver felt the flow of liquid light begin to transfer to the glove. As the energy left his glove there was a flash of sparks where it touched the Dauru.

Afraid for the creature, Oliver started to pull his hand away, but Aethel grabbed it tight. The sparks burst into a heatless flame that slowly encased the creature, licking at it hungrily. Oliver tried to speak but the face of the creature turned to him, features he hadn't seen before brought to light by the moon fire. A nearly human face of countless years and depthless wisdom. There was great pain etched into it and molten tears flowed freely down its face as Oliver tried to dislodge his hand to stop the burning.

A whisper filled his thoughts, "Stop struggling, dear one. I am meant to do this. It was my choice, do not regret it, it is for you and this world." A cry of intense loss followed and Oliver arched his back in responding pain. "Look to the moonlight and you will find your way," breathed the creature. A flash of darkness spread across its face and the flames began to recede. The fire of the being itself followed the moon fire as it sank back into his glove. Within seconds all that remained of Aethel were simmering ashes that quickly dissipated with the wind.

Shocked and crying, Oliver stood and shivered, the moon energy now locked away again. He pressed the thumb stud again in an attempt to bring the creature back into being but as he did so the light coalesced into a shimmering field of glowing points. It hung before him, a vertical chart of sorts, the night sky showing through it. Cold realization hit him and he sank to his knees. This was the celestial map that Aethel had found. He had believed it to be a physical thing but it had been locked inside the creature. The moon energy had somehow taken the map, along with Aethel, into itself.

He groaned as he rolled back and forth on the cold ground. The one that he had thought would guide him, the one he had hoped would take this burden from him, was gone.

He held his head as he tried to force himself to think. What was he to do, his knowledge of stars and their systems was little. He had felt so close to the completion of his quest. Now it stretched outside the limits of his imagination.

Unexpectedly, a conversation he had once had with Magnus filled his mind. In answer to a question regarding the planetary system, he had said, "True understanding of this topic must come with the seeing of its subjects."

Oliver rose unsteadily to his feet and began to make his way back to the others. They had to return to Sun Fire and use the telescope that lay dormant in the tower.

22
MIST STALKERS

Ethan bent over his old friend and willed him to survive. As the first rays of the new day's sun broke, Altameaus lay on a cot in a tent that had been transformed into a medical facility. Ethan knew it was a miracle he breathed at all with the weight that had crushed him.

After the giant creature had been killed, the remainder of the smaller enemy had fled back into the darkness. Their task had been completed. The Seeker weapon on the right of the gorge was a blackened husk, the crystal melted into the ground. The explosion that had awakened Ethan had been caused by the ignition of the solar energy stored in the machine as the wooden frame had burned around it.

Initially, Altameaus had opened his eyes and had even been able to speak, but shortly after had gone comatose. Other Seekers moved busily around the tent as they worked to revive their leader. They had ringed his body with moonstones and their glowing heat filled the small space.

Listening to the whispered discussion around him, Ethan did not feel heartened.

A massive form filled the tent's doorway as Blash bent to look in. "Ah, Ethan, here you are. How is our good friend?" Noting the look on Ethan's face he shook his head, "I have need of you outside. There is little you can do here." He held out a sword he had found to replace Ethan's broken one.

The latent urgency in his voice made Ethan grab the blade and hurry outside. He found Rekin and Rylr there talking with two footmen. He asked, "What is the news?"

Rekin turned and saluted quickly, "Sir, these men are of the sentries sent to the far side of the wood. Movement has been seen to the East and a cloud of darkness follows." He glanced to the sentries for confirmation of his words and received short nods in reply.

Blood began to pound as it flowed through Ethan's veins. Anger towards their enemy surged as he began to spit out orders.

Within minutes his men has taken their positions once more. This time the line across the gorge was only one man deep. Ethan and Blash had made the decision to keep the number of crossbowmen intact, transferring footmen to the task.

Cries of horror suddenly rang through the trees ahead and soon the sentries could be seen running towards them. Some did not stop when they reached the defensive line but continued running, faces pale with fear.

The cries faded into a pervasive silence. Captain Rekin ran to the bluff heights and strained to see an approaching force. He saw nothing but a dark mist that was just making its way into the trees on the far side. Where the mist went, trees and brush trembled as with the movement of many creatures.

As Rekin headed back down to report this to Ethan, the leading tendrils of mist seeped out of the trees and into the open. He and many others clamped down on a urge to cry out. Out of the dark woods shuffled scores of familiar forms.

Human bodies lurched towards the watching soldiers. Their movements were jerky as if moved by another and many had large wounds that had recently bled. Some were missing limbs and limped or crawled as they went. Faces gray and slack, their eyes were closed. A mist moved among them, more alive than the puppets it seemed to control.

Ethan stood locked in place as the things continued their slow progress across the open ground. What was happening? He had expected another rush of the black creatures, not this. He looked to Rylr and then to Rekin as he ran up and their faces reflected the confusion and horror that he felt.

A startled and agonized cry rang out from Ethan's left and the entire force turned to see one of the footmen staggering towards the approaching forms. The soldiers to either side of the man tried to hold him back but he broke free and ran, sobbing a name over and over. Ethan was about to command that he be brought back when the soldier stopped just in front of the animated bodies and sank to his knees. He held out his arms to one of the forms, a woman that must have once been a loved one.

The woman continued the slow jerking movements until past the footman, now surrounded by the initial wave of bodies. The forms stopped as one and turned towards the soldier. His comrades watched, stricken with horror as the things tore out his throat, his screams ending in seconds.

The bodies resumed their slow walk towards Ethan and his men, the body of the footman left behind. As the lines grew closer Rylr caught sight of a tall thin creature darting out of the woods behind the human walkers and called out to the command. Attention arrested from the approaching horde, the soldiers saw the creature, a thing not unlike the beasts of the day before, though thin and wearing robes cinched close. They all watched as it bent over the body of the now dead soldier and poured something into what was left of his throat.

The creature then came to its feet, lifting the body of the dead soldier with it. Steadying the body, it reached into a pocket in its robes and brought out a long cylinder. It broke it in two and a stream of the familiar mist flowed from it, encasing the body. A spasm ran through the footman and the creature stood back as the dead body moved to join its brethren.

Ethan tried not to look the walkers in the face as he gripped his sword until the leather of his gloves cracked under the pressure. He steeled himself to the killing of the people he had once been sworn to protect. "These people are no longer under our protection, they are no more of this world!" He called out to his men to steady them for what was required.

Nearly to the line of soldiers the mist above the dead began to dissipate and the jerking movement ceased. The bodies wavered as if close to collapse and the soldiers looked at each in surprise. Before they could think to do anything but watch, a full dozen of the creatures similar to the one they had seen resurrect their comrade, ran out of the wood line. Sensing a threat, Blash ordered the crossbowmen to fire. Only half of the lithe monsters made it into the ranks of the dead but as they did, they tossed handfuls of the same cylinders amongst the bodies.

Billows of the vaporous mist rose and reached out to cover the horde once more. Immediately the movement continued, the few remaining creatures darting among the sluggish bodies, distributing the mist where it was needed most.

The first ranks of the dead met the soldiers in a thud of metal on flesh. Unarmed, the walking dead kept coming, attempting to overwhelm single footmen. Some, unwilling to strike down what had so recently been innocent countrymen and women were pulled to their deaths.

Mentally bracing himself, Ethan leapt into the mass of animated bodies, sword severing multiple heads at once. The captains to either side followed his charge, screaming their frustration at the senseless killing. Ethan found himself face to face with one of the controlling creatures and smashed his left gauntlet into its face before it could dart away, his sword finishing the job as he continued deeper into the chaos.

Above, Blash focused the archer's fire on the black creatures with the mist. One by one, his men found their targets until one remained, though it was shortly killed by a Seeker using solar dust and stave. Calling for them to cease fire due to the proximity of the soldiers in the low ground, Blash paced back and forth, spittle running down his chin as he ground his teeth in frustration.

Without the creatures spreading the mist, the edges of the vapor slowly receded as the battle raged. One by one the bodies lost their animation and crumpled to the ground. After long agonizing minutes the entire horde was reduced to heaps of limp carcasses. Piles lay around the few soldiers that had succumbed to the horror of the attack.

Ethan slowly made his way through the great piles of dead and silently met with his captains farther up the slope. All he wanted to do was rage and cry against the inhumanity that he had been forced to be a part of but he held himself steady. His men needed an example before they fell apart as well. "Gather the men twenty paces back from the line and have them clean their weapons and ready themselves. I am afraid this will not be the last horror we see today."

Even as he spoke cries of surprise and anger rang out behind them. Realization ran cold through him. The enemy forces had used the dead as a diversion, likely using the time to bring other creatures onto the highlands by smaller, far off passes. He broke into a run up the gorge, his men trailing behind.

The bellows of Blash could be heard throughout the ravine as his hammer crushed one by one the large black armored creatures that now attacked the heights. The majority of the remaining Seekers had been with those on the heights and they fought to protect the crossbowmen that had been ambushed from behind.

Reaching the summit, Ethan gulped in a breath as a wave of black forms filled his vision. As far as he could see to the left and right along the ridgeline were masses of the creatures fighting to get at the humans. Already they had destroyed the remaining solar machine and were even now threatening the tent that housed the wounded. It was ringed by footmen and Seekers, Blash holding the tide at bay at its opening.

Ethan looked back at the soldiers running to join him from below and his throat constricted. The tree line below teemed with more of the creatures. His command was encircled and vastly outnumbered but he did not hesitate. Wrenching his sword free, he charged the enemy that were flinging themselves against the defenders around the tents.

All became a blur of pain and regimented movement. A two-handed slice to the right, a parry above and behind going into a single hand thrust. Bodies of the creatures piled around him, unable to touch him in his fluid dance of destruction. He had nearly made it to the tents and could see the form of Blash intermittently through the wrestling forms when the numbers began to overwhelm him.

Blows began to find their way past his defenses and blood flowed from numerous cuts, sapping his strength until his sword became too heavy to lift. Dropping it, he replaced the weapon with his short sword and continued raining blows on the pressing enemy. As his blows became weaker, the creatures began to hold back, moving out of his reach.

Forming a circle they seemed to wait until he tired. Soon enough he fell heavily to his knees, sword clattering to the ground beside him. Ethan knew it was over. With the backdrop of the frenzied sounds of battle, a creature stalked up and raised its weapon. Blackness sucked him away.

AFTERWARDS

THE CREATURE FELL MADE its way through the silent tunnels beneath Astar Terrace. Taking turns and choosing doors one after another it delved deeper into the earth. The creature finally paused before a metal clad door bolted into the limestone that made up the tunnel. Taking out a key, Fell opened it on grating hinges and stepped through to a stairway that twisted as it dropped away into the darkness.

Fell took the spiraled stair as fast as it could, the air becoming stale in these depths. The stairs ended at a rock wall and Fell placed its hands in an alcove to the side and pulled a hidden lever. The wall swung bringing with it a rush of air. Because air could not naturally make it to this level it had to be pumped down by huge bellows, machines that drew air from the surface and forced it down mile long fissures in the ground.

Stepping through the space left by the opening of the wall, Fell grabbed a torch that lay in a rack nearby and lit the oiled cloth. Metal and glass gleamed in the flickering light as Fell walked down the long hall filled with beakers, sharp metal implements, and steel containers. Tables stretched out of the little light the torch gave and the space went on and on until Fell came to a huge cylinder that stood on end. It had a door in its side and steam hissed softly in rhythmic cadence from tubes and openings in its sides. Shivers of anticipation that it had never been able to control ran up and down Fell's spine. Holding the torch up to a small opening covered in thick transparent quartz, the hunched figure looked in.

A YOUNG GIRL PEERED FROM behind the sacks of grain that had been her home for the last few days. Disheveled brown hair framed a pixie face, now streaked with dirt. Hearing steps nearby, she threw herself back into her hiding place and huddled in the dark, waiting. The sounds faded and she leapt from the sacks and packing crates towards a doorway across the narrow hallway.

Sneaking through the entrance she found herself in the galley. Using the empty sack she carried everywhere, she filled it with molding bread and several slices of cheese that lay on a counter. Moving quickly she headed back towards the door, grabbing a gallon sized barrel of water. She had just placed a foot in the hallway when a shout rang out!

Startled, she dropped her loot and darted into the darkness of the large storage area. Her breath came in gasps as the girl listened for the inevitable pursuit. None came. Eventually her hunger gave her enough courage and she peered over the protective cover. There were none of the hulking black monsters, there were not even any of the many hard-faced men that seemed to operate the ship that rose and fell beneath her.

Taking a breath, she dashed to the scattered provisions she had left in the hallway, gathered them quickly and darted breathlessly back into safety.

Gnawing on the hard bread she tried to relax, sinking back against the sacks that filled this half of the ship's cargo space. Soon her eyes began to droop as weariness pulled her towards sleep. She fought it, knowing what sleep might bring. Black red-eyed faces, like the ones of the creatures that roamed the ship, haunted her dreams. Then there were the moans of pain that emanated from nearby rooms that she knew to be bolted from without. They wormed into her dreams until she would wake herself up doing the same.

Only the hope of one dream finally allowed her to stop resisting and fade into the sleep her small body desperately needed. She dreamed of a woman with flowing light brown hair. She had the light of the ocean in her gray-green eyes and her smile always warmed the girl. Fading into the dream she desperately held to the words the woman sang, "Lucy, my darling, find peace in this night. My Lucy, my joy, no danger in sight."

The stowaway girl named Lucy sighed in her sleep as she sank into deep slumber, the groans of pain left behind.

TRI-ISLAND PEOPLE GROUPS

ASTAR: The self-proclaimed rulers of the Tri-Islands, they are descendants of the original human races to first to come from across the Beryl Sea. The current ruling family traces their lineage back over many centuries. They take great pride in being "pure blood", a term used to raise them above the common man. They are primarily a militant race, placing the art of battle and the path of a warrior higher than anything else.

OSKARA: Handpicked Knights who fill the coveted position of protectors of the land. Unmatched in battle they are looked upon by the Astar people as the backbone of their military might. Lauded as heroes and lords, they are supplied with the best armor and weapons forged in the Western hills by the famed Goblin blacksmiths. They also act as Astar Footmen (common soldiers) troop commanders in time of open war. The three tomes of Oskara aspiration, Control, Honor, and Mastery are the framework of the rigorous training apprentice Oskara go through before being named Knights. Only experienced Oskara Knights who have become skilled in specific tomes are named to be Weapon Masters and are the trainers of new recruits.

SEEKERS: Famed scholars of the study of solar generated power, they revere science, delving into the fabric of nature in their attempts to understand and harness forms of energy. Historically they have provided limited support to the closely related Astar during past wars across the Islands. Their mastery of science and the machines they create are coveted by all, though most are kept secret. They are a reclusive group who rarely leave the Sun Fire Citadel located on an island in the middle of Lake Solari.

GOBLINS: Rock dwellers that inhabit the hill country in the west, they are a peaceful people that have never willingly entered into the arguments and wars of other nations. Faces blunt with little expression, gray pale skin from cave living, Goblins are short, with the average standing 4.5-5 feet tall. Their height is balanced by their great strength, capable of crushing rock and carrying impossibly heavy loads great distances. They have long arms, heavily muscled, with coarse black braided hair.

BLACKSMITHS: These famous Goblins have handed down their secrets throughout the centuries, keeping the knowledge within the close-knit family structure of the Skahg Clan. The most advanced metal workers of the Tri-Islands, they specialize in the making of armor and weapons that are sold at such a high price that only the Astar military is able to purchase in bulk. Their guarded secrets of metal working and smithing combine to produce the sharpest and most dependable edged weapons and armor that can withstand direct blows.

SAVOQ: A tribal people, the Savoq are a nomadic group located in the arid plateau to the South of Lake Solari. Predominantly arid with scrub brush, the landscape necessitates the constant moving of villages between water sources. The environment dictates their use of layered clothing and flowing robes to negate the heat and wind. The Savoq are known as expert horsemen and they put a high level of importance on the number and quality of their steeds. They are a warring people and many long term blood feuds exist between the tribes.

The Savoq are believers in the spirit world, worshiping what they cannot see. It is understood that a good life leads to a good afterlife and there is a focus on pleasing the gods they serve. Shamans hold the power among the Savoq.

ASH: Little is known of the folk believed to inhabit the mountains of Shadowmyst Island west of the mainland. A few vague tales of feline creatures that live in the trees have been handed down by word of mouth in the more rural villages. The majority of the population of the Tri-Islands believes they are a myth.

ABOUT THE AUTHOR

THE AUTHOR GREW UP in small towns across the country, spending most of his childhood in the foothills of the Ozark mountains of Northwestern Arkansas. Throughout his life his favorite books have been sci-fi and fantasy, anything Tolkien, C.S. Lewis, and Terry Brooks and a little Isaac Azimov. Graduating from college in 2004 he became an Army Infantry and Intelligence Officer and continues to serve to this day. While he was deployed to Iraq for 14 months back in 2007-09 he first began writing with this book in mind. His civilian work includes Intelligence Analysis and providing expertise with military training programs. He now lives in Tampa, Florida with his wife of 8 years, Emily, and his 2 children, Oliver and Lucy. He still cannot believe he finished writing something....

He would love to hear from readers. Email him at marklein12@yahoo.com or connect with him on:

Facebook: www.facebook.com/TheSeekersBurden
Twitter: twitter.com/MarkLein12

Made in the USA
Charleston, SC
07 November 2013